Jake, Liam, and Sarah stood outside, gazing down at a mangled tangle of canvas on the ground. 'No, you're right. It definitely has collapsed,' Liam admitted.

Jake squatted down next to the remains of the tent. It had looked in bad shape when he'd left it last night, but now it was worse than ever. Long strands of prickly branches lay draped across it, their thorns having torn dozens of large holes in the fabric.

Although it didn't seem to have moved, the tent was now partly surrounded by a thorny bush, and half a dozen thin branches seemed to be stabbing through it from below the ground. One particularly sharp piece of wood had speared straight up through Jake's pillow.

'That could have been my head,' he realized. 'If we'd stayed in there I'd be dead.'

'I knew you two were hopeless at tent-building, but even for you this is pretty spectacular,' Sarah said. She looked at Jake and nervously chewed her lip. 'This wasn't just the rain, was it?'

Jake stood up, shaking his head. 'No. Last night . . . I think I saw him.'

'Who?' said Liam.

'You know who,' said Jake.

Liam blinked. 'No I don't, or I wouldn't have asked.' He let out a sudden gasp. 'Unless. Wait. Do you mean . . . *him?*'

Jake nodded. 'Yep.'

'The President of Mexico did this?'

Jake and Sarah shot each other uncertain glances. 'Um, no. The Creeper,' said Jake.

'Right, right, of course,' said Liam. 'That was going to be my next guess.'

'I saw him in the woods in the middle of the night,' Jake said.

'What were you doing in the woods in the middle of the night?' asked Sarah.

Jake blushed. 'Um, just . . . the toilet block seemed quite far away.'

Sarah held up a hand. 'Too much information.'

'Are you sure it was him?' asked Liam.

Jake nodded slowly. 'Do you know anyone else with glowing green eyes?'

Liam rubbed his chin. 'Depends. What shade of green?'

'It was him,' said Jake. 'The Creeper. He's out there somewhere, I know it.'

# OXFORD
## UNIVERSITY PRESS

Great Clarendon Street, Oxford OX2 6DP
Oxford University Press is a department of the University of Oxford.
It furthers the University's objective of excellence in research, scholarship,
and education by publishing worldwide. Oxford is a registered trade mark
of Oxford University Press in the UK and in certain other countries

Copyright © Oxford University Press 2017
Illustrations © Lucie Ebrey 2017

The moral rights of the author have been asserted

Database right Oxford University Press (maker)

First published 2017

British Library Cataloguing in Publication Data

Data available

ISBN: 978-0-19-274730-3

1 3 5 7 9 10 8 6 4 2

Printed in Great Britain

Paper used in the production of this book is a natural,
recyclable product made from wood grown in sustainable forests.
The manufacturing process conforms to the environmental
regulations of the country of origin.

# HACKER MURPHY'S

# CREEPER FILES

# WELCOME TO THE JUNGLE

OXFORD
UNIVERSITY PRESS

# the Larkspur

# CAMPSITE CARNAGE

### Raging storm cuts short school trip.

By our man in town,
**HACKER MURPHY**

A group of local schoolchildren and their head teacher were forced to flee for their lives this week, when the biggest storm to hit Larkspur in decades tore through their campsite, collapsing tents and destroying a number of outbuildings.

The storm, which Larkspur Chronicle weather expert, Alfie Gale, described as 'really big', also caused localized flooding, and many of the group's belongings are believed to have been washed away during the heavy downpour.

Camp leader, Lucy Donoghue, 19, described the storm as being, 'like the whole sky was crying angry tears', before explaining that, 'we all get angry, sometimes',

# Chronicle

*ALL THE NEWS YOU NEED THIS WEEK*

and bursting into a lengthy improvised song about the dangers of bottling up emotions.

'Yes, it was a bit on the blustery side,' said the school's head teacher, Mr Campion, 51. 'And while I firmly believe that students of their age should be sturdy enough to withstand a bit of rain and the odd lightning strike to the head and torso, I knew the PTA would have a field day, so I got them all packed up sharpish.'

While most of the pupils were trying to cope with the storm, three of their classmates claim they were encountering something far worse. Jake Latchford, 13, describes the moment he and his friends were confronted by 'a terrifying monster' they refer to as the Creeper.

## CHAPTER ONE

# HACKER'S WELCOME

It's good that you're reading this. The contents of my Creeper Files might save your life one day, so I'm glad you've picked up this new file and are preparing yourself for whatever horrors might lie ahead.

In case you don't know me, I should probably start by introducing myself. The name's Hacker Murphy. Until recently, I was just an average reporter writing average stories for the decidedly below-average local newspaper, *The Larkspur Chronicle*.

All that changed, though, when I heard about the Creeper. Since then, I haven't been able to focus on supermarket openings and school fêtes, no matter how many times my editor might send me to cover them. There's a much more important story out there just waiting to be uncovered, and although my boss doesn't believe me—yet—I'm determined to shine a light on what's really going on.

Ever since three local schoolchildren stopped half-man, half-plant monster, the Creeper, from taking over the world with his army of potato-people (yes, you read that correctly), I've been chasing down leads trying to find him.

Every lead led only one way, though—to a dead end. No matter where I stuck my nose, or which sources I squeezed, the result was the same. The Creeper, it seemed, had vanished, and I didn't know whether to be relieved or disappointed.

Either way, the emotion was short-lived. Little did I realize, the Creeper was just biding his time, working on his new plan. Like the first, this plan involved using his plant-based powers to manipulate nature. This time, though, the Creeper didn't try to serve up an evil potato army, he was looking to serve up something else: revenge.

Revenge, not just on the three children who had defeated him first time around, but on the whole wide world.

2

And what a truly chilling revenge it was going to be . . .

Your friend,
*Hacker Murphy*

## CHAPTER TWO

# THE CAMPING TRIP

Jake Latchford and his best mate, Liam, stepped back to admire their handiwork. Jake tilted his head left and right, trying to find an angle where the construction before them looked anything like it was supposed to.

'Ta-daa,' said Liam, grinning from ear to ear.

Liam's twin sister, Sarah, leaned past them and stared in wonder at what they'd built. 'What's that supposed to be?' she asked.

'It's a tent, obviously,' Liam said.

'It's inside out,' Sarah pointed out. 'The poles are supposed to be on the inside.'

Jake nodded. 'That's it. I knew there was something not quite right.'

Jake would be the first to admit that he was no

4

expert on tents, or the great outdoors in general, in fact. But when an opportunity to go on the school camping trip had come up, he and his friends hadn't been able to resist.

Not long ago they'd come face-to-foliage with a monstrous creature they'd named the Creeper, and had barely survived to tell the tale. And tell the tale they had, only no one had believed a word of it. In fact, pretty much all their classmates—and even some teachers—had laughed at them. Not surprising, really, considering the tale involved exploding potato-men and a machine that turned people into plants.

After going through all that, a few days relaxing in the wilderness was well-deserved, Jake reckoned. If that meant escaping having to take his dog out, empty the dishwasher, and do all his other chores back home, then so much the better!

It wasn't without its downsides, of course. Accompanying the group on the trip was Mr Campion, their exercise-obsessed head teacher. The good news was, he had arranged for them to do all kinds of fun activities, like abseiling, canyoning, kayaking, and more. The bad news was, he had forced them to meet at the school at 6 *a.m.*, then made them set off on a five-mile hike the moment they'd arrived at the campsite.

Liam had managed to sleepwalk through the hike, and only woke up when they arrived back at camp, just in time for breakfast. Mr Campion had tried to insist everyone only eat fruit and vegetables they foraged from the forest, but Sarah had pointed out that, as they weren't technically in school, his authority was limited, and—much to everyone's delight—had produced several packs of bacon from her rucksack.

Unlike Jake and Liam, Sarah was brilliant at camping. Then again, she was brilliant at most things, so that was no real surprise. She knew how to tie knots, navigate using the stars, and identify animal tracks.

She also knew what a tent was supposed to look like, and it was nothing like the teetering, inside-out jumble of plastic and canvas propped up on the grass in front of them.

'How many times is it you've tried building your tent now?'

'How many days have we been here again?' Liam asked.

'Less than one.'

Liam counted on his fingers. 'Nine times,' he said. 'But we've definitely got it this time.'

Right on cue, the tent collapsed.

'OK, *almost* got it,' Liam corrected.

Jake sighed. 'Maybe we should look at the

instructions?'

'Hush your mouth!' Liam gasped, looking horrified. 'We're *men*, Jake. We don't need instructions! We can build things using instinct alone.'

A gust of wind caught the collapsed tent and swirled it up into a tree. Jake, Liam, and Sarah all stared at it in silence for a while.

'What are your instincts telling you now, then?' Sarah asked.

Liam puffed out his cheeks. 'They're telling me that we should've probably brought a ladder,' he said.

'Hmm. Interesting tent placement,' said a voice from behind them. The tone was annoyingly crisp and proper, with just a hint of amusement dripping from the ends. It was a voice they'd all grown pretty fed-up of over the past few hours.

They turned to find Callum peering at them over the rim of his glasses, a lop-sided smirk on his face. None of them had ever been Callum's number one fan in school, but since they'd told everyone about the Creeper and his potato army, Callum had taken great delight in making fun of them at every opportunity. Out here in the wilderness he was proving to be even more annoying.

'I mean, it's unorthodox,' Callum continued. 'I don't imagine it'd be very comfortable the way it's dangling

**7**

from the branches like that, but each to their own. I suppose it'll keep you safe from any more *potato-men*.' He waggled his arms in a vaguely spooky way, and whispered a ghostly, 'Whooooo!'

'What do you want, Callum?' Jake asked.

'Oh, Jake,' said Callum, still smirking. He gestured over to his own tent. With its climate-adjusting air-conditioning and water-dispersing fabric, it looked like something that belonged on an Arctic expedition. 'What could you possibly give me that I don't already have?'

'A personality?' Sarah guessed.

'Friends?' asked Jake.

'Head lice?' said Liam.

'I don't have head lice!' Jake protested.

Liam shrugged. 'You will once you've shared a tent with me.'

'Aaaaanyway,' said Callum, cutting in. 'Delightful as this is, I came over here not because there's something you can do for me, but because there's something I can do for you.'

'Is it shut up and never talk to us again?' Liam asked. 'Because if it is, I'm very much in favour.'

Callum forced a smile. 'Hilarious,' he said, not laughing. 'No. I want to show you something I found.'

Jake sighed. 'Go on, then, get it over with.'

8

'It's not here,' Callum said. 'It's in there.'

He pointed to an area of the woods where the tall trees had knotted together at the top, plunging the forest below it into near-darkness. Another breeze whistled through the leaves, making the branches around them creak ominously.

'What is it?' Jake asked.

'Come and see for yourself,' said Callum. He turned to walk away, then stopped and glanced back over his shoulder. 'Unless you're all too scared.'

Ten minutes of trudging through prickly bushes and overgrown undergrowth later, Jake, Liam, and Sarah found Callum waiting in a narrow clearing. The trees seemed more gnarled and twisted here, and Jake almost cried out in fright when a hand-like branch made a grab for his shoulder.

'It's just the wind,' Sarah whispered, seeing the shock on Jake's face. 'Just the wind and a normal branch. Nothing to worry about.'

Jake hoped she was right. After their encounter with the Creeper, the monster had sworn he'd be back to take his revenge on them. Venturing out on a camping trip right beside an enormous forest filled with trees, plants, and other foliage, Jake was starting to realize, may not actually have been the best idea.

Still, there was no way he was going to let Callum see he was afraid, so he pushed away the branch, squared his shoulders, and tried his best to look tough.

Liam, on the other hand, was taking a very different approach.

'Eek! Bugs! Get them off!' he yelped, dancing in circles and frantically slapping at his face. A bluebottle was buzzing around him, easily dodging his flailing arms. Every time he tried to slap it, the insect flew away, circled Liam's head, then landed on his face again. As a result, Liam's cheeks were covered in red handprints, and the bluebottle was completely unharmed.

'It's a fly,' said Sarah. 'Calm down.'

'It's a giant killer space fly!' Liam said.

'It isn't,' said Sarah. 'It's just a normal fly. It can't hurt you.'

'Most people would say that about potatoes, too,' Liam pointed out, *thwacking* himself on the forehead. 'And look what happened there.'

'Yeah,' snorted Callum. 'Nothing at all.'

He beckoned for them to follow him through a narrow gap in the trees ahead. Liam and Sarah fell into step behind Jake, picking their way carefully through

**10**

the soggy tangle of grass and weeds.

'You don't think he's going to kill us, do you?' Liam whispered.

'Nah,' said Jake. 'Not all of us, anyway.'

'Probably just you,' Sarah added.

Liam swallowed. 'Ha ha. You're kidding,' he said. His eyes darted between them. 'You are kidding, right?'

Before either of them could answer, Jake stumbled out of the trees and into another clearing. All three of them gasped when they saw what stood ahead of them.

It was a tent. A tent which, by the looks of it, had been there for a very long time. Vines had crept across the canvas, almost completely covering it. The few patches of fabric they could still see were heavy with moss and mould.

The roots of the nearest trees were tangled around the bottom, as if they were holding it down to stop it escaping. It looked as though it had been there for decades, and yet still somehow managed to look better than Jake and Liam's effort.

'What's this?' asked Jake.

'I think it's a tent,' said Liam.

'Well, I mean, obviously it's a tent,' said Jake. 'I meant why show us it?'

Callum shrugged. 'I know you three like weird stuff.' He coughed. '*Potato-men*. I thought you might find it cool. I stumbled upon it when I was exploring earlier. I reckon it must have been here for decades.'

A flicker of something wicked crossed his face, unnoticed by Jake and the others. 'I dare you to open it and look inside,' he said.

'No way!' said Jake.

'Only an idiot would look in there,' scoffed Sarah.

'I'll do it!' chimed in Liam, who never could resist a dare. He elbowed past his sister and best friend, then marched right up to the tent.

'See? Point proven,' Sarah sighed. 'Don't do it. There could be anything in there.'

Liam took hold of the zip. It was a little rusty, but still worked. 'You worry too much, sis,' Liam said. He pulled up the zip. 'What's the worst that could happen?' he asked.

And then he screamed as something reached out from within and dragged him inside.

## CHAPTER THREE

# THINGS GET IN TENTS

'Don't eat me! Don't eat me!' Liam howled, as he tumbled inside the tent. 'Or do it quickly if you must!'

He gasped when he came face-to-face with something from his nightmares. Or, one specific nightmare, at least. It was the one where he found himself naked in class, and everyone started laughing at him. Few of them laughed harder than the boy in front of him. He was laughing now, too.

'Matthew!' Liam said, partly-relieved that a monster hadn't caught him, but a tiny bit disappointed, too. At least monsters were interesting. Matthew, on the other hand, was just Callum's annoying mate, and wasn't very interesting at all.

14

'Guilty as charged!' Matthew giggled, doing that annoying snorting laugh he always did. 'Ooh, you should have seen your face! Joke's on you, sucker!'

Liam looked around at the inside of the tent. It was black with mould and heaving with fat, squirming bugs. The smell was pretty overwhelming, and Liam had to narrow his nostrils to stop himself gagging on it.

'How long have you been waiting in here for?' Liam asked.

'About an hour. Hour and a half, maybe,' said Matthew, still grinning broadly. 'Three, absolute tops.'

Liam shuddered as he watched a centipede creep through Matthew's hair. 'Oh. Well, um, yeah, joke's on me,' Liam said, hurriedly backing out of the tent.

Callum was bent over, his hands on his knees, tears streaming down his face. Liam hoped that Sarah had kicked him somewhere painful, but soon realized they were tears of laughter.

'Oh . . . oh, that was brilliant,' Callum wheezed. 'You know I don't like to blow my own trumpet . . .'

'Yeah, right,' Jake muttered.

'But that was the world's most perfect joke!'

Liam stepped aside to let Matthew crawl out of the tent. Matthew was still beaming broadly, apparently oblivious to the hundred or more creatures which

**15**

wriggled and crept across his entire body.

'They fell for it!' Matthew cheered. He held a hand up to Callum for a high-five. All eyes went to his wrist as something with lots of legs emerged from his sleeve.

Slowly—eeeeever so slowly—Matthew looked down. 'Um,' was all he said at first, finally spotting the mass of beetles, slugs, and spiders which had set up home on him.

'I think you've got a bug on you,' said Sarah.

When Matthew spoke, his mouth made a strange clicking noise, like it had suddenly gone dry. 'Thanks for that,' he whispered. Then, with a scream, he ran into the woods, pulling his jumper over his head as he went.

Callum smirked at Jake and the others, but he was no longer laughing. 'You completely fell for it,' he said, sounding a little less certain than he had a moment ago. He glanced in the direction Matthew had run off in. 'I should probably just . . . I'll go and find him.'

He set off, stopped, shouted, 'Losers!' at Jake, Liam, and Sarah, then turned and ran into the trees.

'That boy has some serious issues,' said Sarah, as they listened to him racing off after his co-pranker.

'I bet Matthew has way more after that,' said Jake.

'Serves him right!' Liam added. 'I thought I was going to get eaten alive in there.'

'By midges, maybe,' said Sarah, as they all turned to examine the tent.

The way the trees and roots had grown around it made the tent almost look like it was part of the forest itself. The moss and mould clinging to the outside had well-camouflaged it, and it was impossible to tell how long it had been there for. Years, certainly. Possibly decades, like Callum had said.

In fact, the tent looked so much a part of the forest, Jake couldn't help but wonder if it had been there even before the trees had.

'Do you think someone lives in it?' Sarah wondered.

'Not unless they're invisible,' said Liam. 'I've just been inside, remember?'

**17**

Sarah rolled her eyes. 'Well *obviously* they're not home right now,' she said. She glanced around at the dark woods surrounding them. 'Maybe they've gone out.'

'Out? To do what?' Liam asked, finding his voice dropped to a whisper without him really planning it.

'To hunt?' said Jake.

Liam blinked. 'What sort of weirdo would live in a mouldy tent full of bugs and go out hunting in the woods?' he asked.

All three of them drew in closer together, their eyes darting across the suddenly sinister-looking trees. 'Not one I'd really like to meet,' said Sarah in a low croak.

Jake swallowed. 'Maybe we should go back to camp,' he said.

'Yes,' said Sarah. 'I think we should definitely do that. Right now.'

'Last one there's a rotten leg!' Liam yelped, then he set off running and plunged into the forest.

Jake and Sarah watched him go. At last, Sarah sighed. 'I suppose we should really tell him he's going the wrong way,' she said.

'Yeah,' said Jake, setting off after his friend. 'Yeah, I suppose we probably should.'

18

Forty minutes later, Jake and Sarah trudged into the camp, with Liam trailing behind them. They were wet, muddy, and each had their fair share of insect bites. Bits of twig were tangled in Sarah's hair, and Liam had a red mark on his face from when he'd run straight into a tree.

The rest of the class had gathered around a campfire. Jake, Liam, and Sarah sat on a log near the back, pretending not to notice Callum sniggering at them. Matthew sat on the ground beside Callum, hugging his own legs and gently rocking back and forth with a haunted look in his eyes.

Matthew seemed to be bug-free now, but every so often he'd let out a little whimper, frantically scratch himself, then go back to rocking again.

'Meet any evil vegetables on your way home?' Callum called over, but before Jake could respond, a man and a woman stepped into the circle and stood either side of the campfire.

Jake had seen them a couple of times since they'd all arrived that morning, but this was the first time he'd paid them much attention. The man was broad and surly-looking, with hair shaved almost all the way down to the bone. He looked like an army drill sergeant, and appeared to scowl as he cast his eye across the assembled group.

The woman, on the other hand, was pretty much his exact opposite. She was about the same height as most of the pupils, with narrow shoulders and blonde hair that stood up in an exaggerated quiff at the front. She had a ring through her nose, and a smile that wouldn't have looked out of place on a TV show for particularly timid pre-schoolers.

A sunshine-yellow guitar was held across her shoulder by a rainbow-coloured strap. As the gathered crowd fell silent, she swung the guitar in front of her and began to strum.

'Hello! Hello! Welcome to our campsite,' she sang in a reedy voice that reminded absolutely everyone present of fingernails scraping down a blackboard. Even the man beside her winced and shuffled further away. 'Hello! Hello! We're gonna have some fun, right?'

'That's a terrible rhyme,' whispered Sarah.

'She can't sing very well, either,' added Jake.

Liam was sitting bolt upright on the log. 'I'm in love!' he declared, as the woman launched into the next verse.

'There's climbing, camping, kayaking too. Here at the camp there's so much to do! Hello, hello, hello!'

She finished with a series of loud, out-of-tune strums, then bowed to what would have been total silence, had Liam not stood up and loudly clapped his approval.

'Encore! Encore!' he cried. 'More of that sort of thing!'

The woman shot him an appreciative smile. Everyone else just stared blankly at him until he sat down again. He cleared his throat, suddenly embarrassed. 'Continue.'

'Hi guys!' the woman said, far too enthusiastically, Jake thought. 'My name's Lucy, and I'm one of the two camp leaders! And now let me introduce you to this guy on my left. Let's all say hello to the one . . . the only . . .'

She spun on the spot and finished with an elaborate pointing motion in the man's direction. He let out an audible sigh of contempt and muttered, 'Dave.'

'Dangeroooous Dave!' Lucy sang.

'And Lovely Lucy,' Liam said.

Sarah shook her head. 'Oh, good grief,' she muttered.

'Just to clarify, I'm not actually dangerous,' said Dave.

'He's *Deadly* Dave!' Lucy said, narrowing her eyes and adding a *dun-dun-duuuun* for dramatic effect.

Dave shook his head. 'I'm not. I'm the opposite of that,' he said, flatly. 'I'm here—both of us—to make sure you stay safe. We've got a whole programme of events for you, which I'm sure you'll find fun,' he explained, although the way his nostrils flared on the word 'fun' suggested he wasn't exactly over the moon about the idea. 'But your safety is our number one priority.'

Lucy nodded. 'Dave's right,' she said, strumming her guitar again. She broke into a warbled song. 'But there's only one rule, and that's to have fun! There are no other rules but that! Enjoy yourself and—'

'There are other rules,' said Dave, with the resigned tone of a man who'd been through this too many times before. 'There are loads of other rules. No fighting, no mucking around, and absolutely no wandering off and getting lost in the woods. And that's just for starters.'

Jake leaned closer to Sarah and Liam. 'He's a barrel of laughs, isn't he?'

'Don't worry, there's no chance Liam could get lost,' said Callum. 'We'd hear his high-pitched screams from miles away!'

'I wasn't screaming!' Liam protested. 'I was whistling.'

Callum snorted. 'You were whistling, "please don't eat me, please don't eat me, I don't want to die"?'

'He's very talented,' said Jake, leaping to Liam's defence.

Lucy threw her arms in the air. 'Whistle-off!' she cried, then she pursed her lips and whistled a tune she had definitely just improvised, because no one would ever write a tune that bad.

She kept whistling for a full minute or more, dancing along to the rhythm, which apparently only she could detect. Dave stood in silence the whole time, his hands in his pockets, his eyes turned to the sky.

'Dave, go!' Lucy cried, when she'd finished. Dave stared at her impassively for a few seconds, before turning back to the group.

'You'll find the full rules on the noticeboard, along with a list of the activities on offer,' he said. 'You are free to choose any activities you like, but make sure you familiarize yourself with the rules first.'

'The most important rule of all is "be happy"!' sang Lucy, twanging the strings of her guitar. 'The most important rule of all is "have fun"! The most important thing to do is to try something that's new . . .'

'Any questions?' asked Dave, shouting to drown out Lucy's singing. 'No? Good,' he said before anyone had a chance to raise a hand, then he turned and marched off, leaving Lucy to murder the final few notes of her song.

'Bravo!' cheered Liam, leaping to his feet again. 'You should be on TV!'

'Yeah, then we could turn the volume down,' Sarah whispered, and Jake had to stifle a giggle.

'So, what do you want to do?' Jake asked, once he'd composed himself.

'Marry that woman,' said Liam, dreamily.

Jake frowned. 'Um, yeah. I meant on the activity front.'

'Oh. Right,' said Liam. He shrugged. 'Don't really mind.'

'Looks like Callum and Matthew are going climbing,' said Sarah, as she watched them pick up ropes and harnesses.

Jake stood up. 'Well, if those two are going climbing, that's settled it,' he said. 'Kayaking it is!'

## CHAPTER FOUR

# A DIP IN THE LAKE

Liam gripped the sides of his kayak and wriggled his legs down into the craft's long, thin body. The kayak bobbed and wobbled on the water, and for a moment Liam was convinced it was going to tip over.

'I'm going to fall in!' he announced.

'No, you aren't,' said Dave, holding the kayak steady. 'Find your balance and you'll be fine. Besides, you've got a life jacket on, so even if you do, what's the worst that'll happen?'

Liam glanced at the water. 'I don't know. Sharks?'

Dave frowned. 'Sharks?'

'Or crocodiles?' Liam guessed. 'I saw a programme about them once. They wait just under the surface then grab you by the ankles and pull you down.'

'Relax. There are no crocodiles or sharks in this water,' Dave reassured him.

'Hippos?' said Liam, his eyes wide in panic. He began to wriggle free of the kayak. 'Maybe I should go and join Lucy's group, just to be on the safe side.'

Dave clamped a hand on Liam's shoulder and shoved him back down. 'You'll be fine. We've been through all the training. Nothing is going to go wrong, trust me. Now off you go.'

Standing up, Dave put a foot on Liam's kayak and shoved it away from the little wooden jetty. Liam flailed wildly with his long double-ended oar, and came dangerously close to *thwacking* Jake on the back of the head with it.

Despite having spent a full hour doing the safety checks and practising, Jake was having some issues with his own kayak, which seemed worryingly unstable. He couldn't quite get the hang of paddling, either, and no matter which direction he turned the blades, he kept going backwards.

Sarah, on the other hand, was gliding smoothly through the water with what seemed to be very little effort whatsoever.

'Sickening, isn't it?' Liam muttered, as Jake drifted backwards past him. 'She's good at everything.'

'Not as sickening as *that*,' said Jake. He nodded

towards the jetty, where Callum was sliding down into a kayak like it was the easiest thing in the world.

Liam groaned. 'I thought he was going climbing.'

'I was,' said Callum, using his paddle to shove himself and his kayak away from the jetty. 'But then I saw you doing this and thought it'd be much more fun to come and watch you muck it up.'

'And I suppose you're an expert?' said Jake.

Callum nodded proudly. 'Under 13s Cross-Channel Champion two years running,' he crowed. From behind him, there came a short scream and a loud splash. Callum's smile didn't so much as flicker. 'Matthew, on the other hand? It's his first time.'

'You see?' said Dave, pointing to where a miserable-looking Matthew was bobbing around in the water. 'This is why we wear life jackets. See how easily it can happen?'

'C-can you g-get me out, please?' Matthew muttered, his teeth rattling together with cold. Dave squatted down, caught him by the back of his bright red life vest, then hoisted him out of the water with one hand.

'Now, then,' Dave said. 'Let's try that again.'

Ten minutes later, the whole group—Jake, Liam, Sarah, Callum, Matthew, and a couple of others—were in their kayaks, paddling along behind Dave. Callum and Sarah were easily keeping pace, while everyone else frantically thrashed the water with their paddles and tried to catch up.

They had set off from a narrow strip of water, but as they paddled around a bend at the bottom of a hill, a wide lake opened up before them. The water seemed to stretch all the way to the horizon—a perfectly still landscape of deep, dark blue.

'Whoa,' said Jake. 'It's ... It's ...'

'Big?' guessed Liam.

'No, it's ...'

'Wet?'

'No! It's amazing,' said Jake. 'It's stunning.'

And it was. The afternoon sunshine bounced off the water's rippling surface, making it shimmer and dance. On either side of the lake stood lush green hills, marked here and there with pockets of trees. Jake felt like he'd paddled straight into a landscape painting.

'It's also big and wet,' Liam pointed out. 'So technically I was correct.'

Dave pulled off a fancy about-turn so his kayak was facing the rest of the group. 'OK, guys, you're free to explore the lake—but remember the rules. Don't go anywhere I can't see you. How will you know if I can see you?'

Liam's hand shot up.

'Yes?'

'If you've got your eyes open.'

'Well ... not quite what I was getting at,' said Dave. 'I was going to say that if you can't see me, then I can't see you.'

Liam's hand shot up again. Dave tried to hide the irritation in his voice, but didn't make a very good job of it. 'Yes?'

'What if we're behind you?' Liam asked. 'We'd be able to see you, but you wouldn't be able to see us.'

'And why would you be behind me?'

Liam thought for a moment. 'If we were playing hide-and-seek.'

Dave blinked slowly. 'Tell you what, don't play hide-and-seek, OK?'

'Gotcha,' said Liam. 'Is that one of the rules?'

'It is now,' said Dave.

Throughout Dave and Liam's conversation, Jake had become distracted by the long green strands of weed wafting around below the water. It was quite hypnotic the way they danced on the current. The way they drifted left and right almost made it look like they were waving up at him.

'Jake?'

Jake jumped, startled by the sound of his name. 'Hmm?'

**29**

'You get all that?' Dave asked.

Jake glanced around at the others. They were all watching him, waiting for him to say something. 'Um, yeah. Got it. Don't go out of sight and . . . all that other stuff. Got it.'

'OK, then. Well, go and have fun,' said Dave. '*Carefully*.'

Dave turned his kayak and paddled ahead towards where the shore curved round in a sweeping bend. Jake and Liam tried to follow, but their complete lack of skills meant they made lots of splashing with very little in the way of movement.

'Terry's getting away!' Liam pointed out.

'Who's Terry?' asked Jake.

'Him. The leader guy,' said Liam.

'You mean Dave?'

'Dave?' Liam frowned.

'Yes.'

'Who's Terry, then?'

'No idea,' said Jake. 'But hurry up and paddle, or we're going to fall behind.'

They flailed with their paddles, but by the time they were even headed in the right direction, Dave was almost out of sight around the corner.

'Avast, ye landlubber!' cried Callum, in a really quite terrible pirate accent.

Jake turned just in time to see Callum's kayak bearing down on him. There was a loud *bump*, a sudden jerk, and Jake barely had time to catch his breath before his kayak rolled and the icy-cold water raced up to meet him.

Even under the water, Jake could hear Callum's braying laughter, as well as the panicked shouts of Liam and Sarah. Hanging upside-down, Jake tried to kick himself free of the kayak, but his right foot was snagged on the inside lining, and there was no room to reach in and unhook it.

Something swished across Jake's face and tangled through his hair. He reached up—or was it down?—to feel for it, then tensed as it wrapped tightly around his wrist.

Forcing his eyes open, Jake saw one of the long, weedy vines tangled around his arm. Another snaked towards him, like it was growing at an incredible rate, reaching for his throat.

With his free arm, Jake tried to bat the weed away, but it weaved through the water, avoiding his arm. Closer and closer it came, reaching for him, grabbing for him, trying to pull him down.

Jake's lungs burned with the effort of holding his breath. The dirty water nipped his eyes. He wanted to scream, but he knew if he opened his mouth, it would all be over.

And then, just before the vine could wrap itself around his throat, the kayak turned. Jake gasped as he broke the surface, and gulped down several deep breaths of air. Liam and Sarah were beside him, each pulling on a length of rope at either end of his kayak as they dragged it back upright.

'It's OK, we got you,' said Sarah.

'What's going on?' called Dave, hurriedly paddling back towards them. 'Jake? Are you OK?'

Jake nodded, still too breathless to speak.

'Good. That's good. But as for *you*,' Dave said, turning his attention to Callum. 'What on earth were you thinking?'

'It was an accident, sir,' said Callum, managing to look completely innocent. 'I just lost control and bumped into him.'

'No, you didn't!' protested Sarah. 'You did it on purpose.'

Callum shrugged. 'Oh yeah? Prove it.'

'Forget it,' said Dave. 'It's over and done with.' He stabbed an accusing finger at Callum. 'Just be sure it doesn't happen again.'

Callum paddled backwards away from the rest of the group. 'OK, sir. I'd hate for poor Jake to get all wet and frightened again.' He let out a loud cackle. 'Come on, Matthew, let's leave these drips to it.'

**33**

'I really hate him sometimes,' Sarah mumbled, as they watched Callum paddle off across the lake.

'Funny,' said Liam. 'I really hate him all the time.'

Jake coughed, and a piece of mulchy green weed the size of his tongue was ejected out of his mouth and back into the water. 'Yeah,' he wheezed. 'I'm not his greatest fan, either.'

It took Jake and Liam just over three hours to get the hang of kayaking. They had finally mastered how to go forwards without wobbling around when the activity ended, and Dave guided them all to shore.

Back at camp, Lucy had fired up the barbecue, and the rest of the class were gathered around a campfire, tucking into overcooked burgers and charcoaled sausages.

Mr Campion, who had spent the day scaling three nearby mountains with his bare hands, sat on a log, looking deeply dismayed by the amount of junk food being munched on.

'Trust me on this—your colons will not thank you for that stuff,' he warned. He held up an oval-shaped ball of tinfoil and began to peel away the edges. 'This is

**34**

the type of campfire fare you want to be eating.'

The head teacher opened the ball of foil and Liam let out a squeal of terror when he spotted the fat, crispy baked potato lurking within. Instinctively, he kicked the spud out of Mr Campion's hands, sending it sailing across the camp, before it exploded against a tree with a *splurt*.

Mr Campion stared in the direction the spud flew.

He stared at his hands.

He stared at Liam.

'Sorry,' Liam said. 'I thought it was going to kill us.'

'It was a potato,' said Mr Campion.

'Exactly,' Liam said, nodding. 'Better safe than sorry, eh?'

Sarah put an arm around Liam's shoulder and smiled down at Mr Campion. 'He's tired,' she explained, gently leading her brother away. 'Too much excitement for one day.'

They sat down on another log beside Jake, who was already halfway through his first hot dog and eyeing up a second. The evening was drawing in, and the flames from the campfire cast flickering shadows across the faces of the other kids.

Lucy appeared in front of them, a set of tongs in one hand and a spatula in another. 'Now, what can I do for you?'

**35**

'Marry me,' said Liam, then he clamped his hand over his mouth. Had he just said that out loud?!

Jake choked on his hot dog, then hurriedly swallowed it down. 'With a burger,' he wheezed. 'He means marry him with a burger.'

Lucy frowned. 'Marry him with a burger?'

'I know, it's weird, isn't it?' said Jake, laughing a bit too loudly. 'It's just the way he says stuff. *Marry me with a burger, get me engaged to a strawberry milkshake*, um . . . *celebrate my silver wedding anniversary with a cake.* It's just the way he asks for food.'

Lucy's frown deepened even further. 'Why?'

'He's clinically insane,' said Sarah. Liam shot her an accusing look, but then nodded slowly, his hand still pressed against his mouth.

'Um, well, OK then,' said Lucy. She brightened, her smile returning. 'Proposal accepted! One meat-marriage coming right up!'

Liam pulled his hand away. 'I'm clinically insane? What did you go and say that for?'

'Sorry,' Sarah giggled. 'Just came out.'

'And you probably are,' Jake added.

'Yeah, fair point,' Liam conceded. 'Hey, where did you get that?' he asked, spotting a small red object in Sarah's hand.

'What, this?' she said, holding up a small Swiss

Army knife. 'Dad gave it to me.'

Liam's jaw dropped. 'What? He gave you a *knife*? Why didn't he give me a knife?'

'Well, to be fair, you can barely be trusted with a spoon,' said Sarah. 'Which this also has, by the way.'

She flicked a little spoon-shaped attachment from the handle to demonstrate. 'See? It's also got corkscrews, can openers, nail files . . . it's pretty handy.'

'Can I have it?' Liam asked.

Sarah slipped the knife into her pocket. 'No,' she said. 'You'll only go and accidentally chop your arm off.'

'Yeah,' Liam grunted. 'You're probably right.'

Later, once Liam had been given his burger's hand in marriage, and most of the other food had been gobbled up, Mr Campion strode into the centre of the circle. He inhaled deeply through his nose, puffing his chest up like a gorilla.

'Smell that?' he said.

'Sorry, sir, that was me,' said Liam. 'That last burger didn't agree with me.'

A ripple of laughter went round the circle. Mr Campion glared at Liam, but did his best to laugh it off. 'Ha, ha, ha, yes,' he said, drily. 'I meant the fresh air. There's nothing quite like it. Getting out into the wilderness, gathering round the campfire.'

He cast his gaze slowly across the faces around him.

'Telling ghost stories,' he said, and the laughter was replaced by a low murmuring.

'I remember my first camping trip,' Mr Campion said, his voice a hushed whisper. 'It was a night much like this one, in a place a lot like here.'

The flames flickered on the breeze, casting spooky shadows across the head teacher's face. 'It was a night I will never forget. A night when I discovered the true meaning of terror . . .'

## CHAPTER FIVE

# WEE WORRIES

Liam wriggled into his sleeping bag and pushed the sagging side of the tent away from his head. It immediately flopped back down again and pressed against his face. It had taken almost twenty minutes to get the tent out of the tree, and another forty to put it back together.

Although *back together* was a pretty generous description for it. The tent looked like it had been trampled by a herd of wildebeest. It was so out of shape, the boys couldn't even be sure if it was the right way up. For all they knew, the whole thing might be inside out.

Jake flopped down in his sleeping bag and sighed. 'We so should have followed the instructions.'

'Jake, please,' said Liam. 'There's nothing wrong with the tent.'

'There's nothing right with it, you mean,' said Jake. 'It isn't even pegged down. The only thing stopping it blowing away is us.'

'Then well done us, I say,' said Liam. He pushed the flopping side of the tent away again. 'What did you think of Mr Campion's ghost story?'

Jake wrinkled his nose. 'Meh. Wasn't really a ghost story, was it? It was really just a lecture on healthy eating he vaguely tried to disguise as a ghost story.'

'Yeah,' Liam agreed. 'I stopped listening when he revealed the ghost was actually Type 2 Diabetes.'

Jake shrugged. 'He's a grown-up. They don't believe in ghosts and monsters. Not really.'

'Yeah,' Liam agreed. 'But we know different, don't we?'

'Yeah,' said Jake. 'Yeah, we do.'

They lay in silence for a while, listening to the rustling of leaves and the creaking branches of the trees outside. Liam had broken the door zip approximately eight seconds after they'd first unpacked the tent, and the wind whistled as it came in through the gaps.

'I really hope it doesn't rain,' Jake said.

Liam rolled over in his sleeping bag. 'Don't worry,' he said. 'It won't. Trust me, I know these things.'

Two hours later, Jake woke up in a puddle. He opened his eyes just in time to see a fat drip of water trickle down the inside of the tent, then drop onto his forehead. Outside, the swishing of leaves had been replaced by the rat-a-tat rattle of raindrops on canvas.

Jake sat up and glanced at Liam, who was fast asleep and snoring soundly. 'So, not going to rain, is it?' he mumbled. 'I'm really glad you know these things.'

'There's a shark in my legs!' Liam announced. 'It's after the jam!'

There was a moment of silence, then Liam returned to snoring again. Despite being damp, cold, and uncomfortable, Jake couldn't help but laugh.

'He's even weirder when he's asleep,' Jake whispered.

His sleeping bag squelched as he lay back down. He wriggled around, trying to find a comfortable position, but there was a rock or a tree root right underneath him which made it impossible. He couldn't remember it being there earlier, but maybe he was just too tired to notice at the time.

A more pressing problem was developing. The sound of all that rainwater running down the tent was making Jake realize he needed a wee. In fact, he *really* needed a wee.

Right now!

Kicking out of his sleeping bag, Jake clambered along the tent and crawled onto the soaking wet ground. The rain lashed at him, and he was thankful that he'd decided to sleep in his clothes, and not the thin cotton pyjamas his mum had packed him off with.

The campfire was now just a smouldering bundle of glowing embers, but there were a couple of battery-operated lamps hanging from trees to try to push back the worst of the darkness.

The toilet blocks were on the other side of the camp, and Jake wasn't convinced he'd make it in time. He turned towards the trees, then jumped back when he saw how close they were. The branches stretched out towards the tent, twigs splayed like grabbing fingers. Had they pitched the tent this close to the woods? Or had it moved during the night?

Jake felt a shudder travel down his spine. Maybe the tent hadn't moved. Maybe the trees had . . .

'Get a grip,' he whispered, giving himself a shake. He stumbled towards the closest lamp, then carried on past it into the trees.

Hurriedly, he fiddled with the button of his trousers, tucked himself in behind a clump of bushes, and let rip.

'Aaaah,' he mumbled, letting out a sigh of relief. That had been a little too close for comfort. Mind you, his sleeping bag was already soaked through, so even if he had wet himself, he probably wouldn't have noticed.

Just as he finished and fastened his button again, Jake heard a rustling through the trees behind him. He turned and peered into the darkness, and for a moment he thought he saw . . . something. A shape, maybe. A flicker of movement.

From over on his left there came the snapping of a twig. Jake spun, his heart crashing in his chest, his blood whooshing through his veins. 'Hello?' he said in a low croak. 'Liam, is that you?'

Another sound. To his right, this time. A hissing, like a whisper on the wind. 'Jaaaaaake,' it seemed to say. 'Jaaaaaake.'

'Callum? If that's you, this isn't funny,' Jake said, then he yelped as something exploded from the woods beside him.

Jake threw up his hands for protection as the thing hurled itself towards him. He ducked just in time

**43**

for a bird to go swooping up into the treetops behind him, and almost laughed with relief when he heard the annoyed *hooting* of an owl from up in the branches.

'Sorry if I peed on your house,' Jake said. 'But you almost gave me a heart attack, so I'd say we're pretty much even now.'

He turned around, looking for the glow of the lamp that would lead him back to camp, but all around him was nothing but shadowy darkness. The only light came from the faint glow of the moon through the gaps in the trees—gaps which seemed to be getting narrower with every second that passed.

'Great,' Jake muttered, searching around for something he recognized. In the moonlight, though, all the trees looked the same, and there was nothing to tell him which direction led back to his tent.

There was a creaking of branches behind him. Jake turned, expecting to see the owl moving around in the treetops, but instead he saw something that made a scream bubble up at the back of his throat.

Eyes.

Two piercing green eyes watched him through the forest's foliage.

The darkness around the eyes moved, taking the shape of a tall, terrifying figure. The Creeper. It had to be!

Jake ran, pushing his way through the tangled knots of branches that seemed to claw at him as he passed. The forest became a twisting maze around him, growing darker and darker as he zig-zagged frantically through it.

Where was the camp? *Where was the camp?* He couldn't see anything that might show him the way.

But then he heard something. It was, just for that moment, his most favourite sound in the whole world.

It was the sound of Liam snoring!

Turning sharply, Jake stumbled in the direction of the sound. Thin branches whipped at his face. Roots seemed to snag at his feet, as if trying to drag him down. He jumped and hopped the last few metres, then tumbled out of the trees and rolled to a stop in the puddle beside his tent.

On a nearby branch, the lantern flickered into life again. Jake lay on his back, panting heavily and scanning the forest for any sign of those eerie green eyes, but the Creeper was nowhere to be seen.

Getting to his feet, Jake wiped the mud from his face and picked the leaves from his hair. The rain had stopped, but the storm had taken its toll on the tent, which had now completely collapsed on top of the snoring Liam. 'I'm made of hats!' Liam announced, mid-snort. His voice was muffled by the canvas on top of him. 'Don't let the chicken drink the table.'

Jake shook his head and peered back into the woods again. There was still no sign of anyone watching him, and now that he wasn't running in panic, he started to wonder if he'd imagined the whole thing. Maybe Mr Campion's ghost story had affected him more than he'd thought.

Even if it had been the Creeper, there was no sign of him now. The sensible thing would be to try to get some sleep, Jake knew, but there was no way he could spend the rest of the night lying in a puddle. Even without Liam's snoring, and a possible monster on the loose, getting to sleep in the collapsed tent was going to be impossible.

There was only one thing for it. Only one possible solution.

Jake drew in a deep breath and steeled his nerve.

What he was about to do was awful. Horrifying.

But there was no other choice.

## CHAPTER SIX

# THE COLD LIGHT OF DAY

'Psst.'

Jake listened outside the tent, waiting for some sort of response. When none came, he tried again.

'Psst. Sarah. Can we sleep in your tent tonight?'

The thought of sharing a tent with a girl horrified him, but he didn't see what other choice there was. At this point, his and Liam's tent wasn't really a tent at all. It was more like a burst water bomb.

Besides, Sarah wasn't a *proper* girl. Not really. She was Jake's friend and Liam's sister, so that cancelled any girly qualities out.

'Psst. Sarah!'

'What?' Sarah snapped, pulling up the tent zip in

one sudden tug. Her eyes were half-closed, and her hair looked like a stick of candyfloss.

'Can we sleep in here tonight? Our tent's fallen down.'

Sarah yawned, shrugged, and screwed up her eyes at the same time. She gave a grunt that Jake took to mean, 'yes', then she lay back down and fell asleep before Jake could tell her about his possible Creeper sighting.

'Thanks,' he whispered, then he returned to his own tent, grabbed hold of Liam's feet through his sleeping bag, and dragged him across the wet ground.

'You can't trust mustard,' Liam mumbled, as his head bumped across the uneven ground. 'It's made of wasps.'

With a combination of shoving, dragging, and rolling, Jake managed to get Liam into Sarah's tent. Doubling back, he got his own sleeping bag and wrung most of the water out of it. His pillow was a soggy mess, though, so he decided to leave it where it was.

Sarah's tent was meant for four people, so there was plenty of room for him to unroll his sleeping bag once he'd climbed inside. He hesitated before zipping the door closed, and glanced around at the shadowy trees. He saw nothing staring back at him, and as he pulled the zip closed he felt a huge sense of relief wash over him. Maybe he'd imagined those eyes watching him.

'Yeah,' he whispered. 'Maybe.'

And before he could think about it too much more, Jake slipped inside his sleeping bag, rested his head on his hands, and did his best to fall asleep.

Next morning, Jake woke up to find Sarah staring down at him. 'Why are you two in my tent?' she demanded.

'You said we could,' Jake reminded her.

Sarah's eyes narrowed. 'Did I?'

'Yes!' said Jake. 'Well, I mean, you made a sort of grunting noise, so I took that to mean we could.'

A flicker of recollection passed across Sarah's face. 'You woke me up,' she said. 'Something about your tent.'

'It collapsed,' said Jake. The memory of those emerald-green eyes reared up again. 'And there was something else, too ...'

'He's a detective horse!' roared Liam, sitting upright so suddenly he looked like he was spring-loaded. He yawned, rubbed his eyes, then flopped back down and started snoring again.

'Does he always do that?' Jake asked.

Sarah shrugged. 'Not those exact words, but yeah,' she said. She gave her brother a shake. 'Liam.'

Liam kept snoring.

'Liam. Liam. Liam.'

She shook him harder.

'Liam.'

She flicked his ear.

'Liam. Liam. *Liam.*'

Liam *still* kept snoring.

'Leave this to me,' said Jake. He cleared his throat. 'Breakfast's ready,' he said, in a voice that was barely above a whisper. Liam opened his eyes and sat up.

'Nice!' he said. 'I'll have some bacon, if it's going.'

He glanced around him and blinked in surprise. 'See, Jake? There's nothing wrong with the tent. It's perfect!'

'That's because it's mine,' said Sarah. 'Yours completely collapsed.'

Liam shook his head and laughed. 'Oh, I doubt that very much!'

Two minutes later, Jake, Liam, and Sarah stood outside, gazing down at a mangled tangle of canvas on the ground. 'No, you're right. It definitely has collapsed,' Liam admitted.

Jake squatted down next to the remains of the tent.

It had looked in bad shape when he'd left it last night, but now it was worse than ever. Long strands of prickly branches lay draped across it, their thorns having torn dozens of large holes in the fabric.

Although it didn't seem to have moved, the tent was now partly surrounded by a thorny bush, and half a dozen thin branches seemed to be stabbing through it from below the ground. One particularly sharp piece of wood had speared straight up through Jake's pillow.

'That could have been my head,' he realized. 'If we'd stayed in there I'd be dead.'

'I knew you two were hopeless at tent-building, but even for you this is pretty spectacular,' Sarah said. She looked at Jake and nervously chewed her lip. 'This wasn't just the rain, was it?'

Jake stood up, shaking his head. 'No. Last night . . . I think I saw him.'

'Who?' said Liam.

'You know who,' said Jake.

Liam blinked. 'No I don't, or I wouldn't have asked.' He let out a sudden gasp. 'Unless. Wait. Do you mean . . . *him?*'

Jake nodded. 'Yep.'

'The President of Mexico did this?'

Jake and Sarah shot each other uncertain glances. 'Um, no. The Creeper,' said Jake.

'Right, right, of course,' said Liam. 'That was going to be my next guess.'

'I saw him in the woods in the middle of the night,' Jake said.

'What were you doing in the woods in the middle of the night?' asked Sarah.

Jake blushed. 'Um, just . . . the toilet block seemed quite far away.'

Sarah held up a hand. 'Too much information.'

'Are you sure it was him?' asked Liam.

Jake nodded slowly. 'Do you know anyone else with glowing green eyes?'

Liam rubbed his chin. 'Depends. What shade of green?'

'It was him,' said Jake. 'The Creeper. He's out there somewhere, I know it.'

The three friends drew closer together and stared into the woods. The forest didn't look nearly as creepy in the early morning sunlight, but there was still something ominous about the deep shadows and twisted trees.

'Still, if it really is the Creeper,' Sarah whispered, 'at least we know what he looks like in human form. He won't be able to trick us again.'

'Great! I'll take comfort in that when the trees are ripping our arms and legs off,' said Liam, shooting worried looks at the gnarled branches.

'What on earth happened here?' demanded a voice from behind them. They all yelped in fright, then spun around to find Lucy standing over the wrecked tent.

'It was the rain,' said Jake.

'It made the tent collapse,' added Sarah.

'Totally not our fault,' said Liam, smoothing down his hair and offering Lucy his most charming smile.

Lucy smiled back and reached around to her back. For the first time, Jake realized she had her guitar with her. She twanged the strings tunelessly as she swung the instrument in front of her. 'Let's sing a song about re-spons-ibility, re-spons-ibility, re-spons-ibility,' she warbled. 'I know a song about re-spons-ibility, and this is how it goes . . .'

Several verses, three choruses, and what felt like an unnecessarily long guitar solo later, Lucy took a bow. Only Liam clapped, and even then it was mostly through relief that the song was over.

'So, what have we learned?' Lucy asked, swinging the guitar onto her back again.

'That you never took guitar lessons?' said Liam.

Lucy beamed. 'That's right. Completely self-taught! But I meant what did we learn about responsibility?'

'That it doesn't really rhyme with very much?' guessed Jake.

'That they need to take some for themselves,' said Sarah. 'That they should have been more responsible when putting up their tent, and now they have to live with the consequences.'

'Exactly!' said Lucy. 'This week is all about learning to look after yourself, so it wouldn't be very good if I just gave you a new tent, would it?'

'It'd be *quite* good,' said Jake, hopefully.

'No,' said Lucy, shaking her head. 'You guys are just going to have to put up with not having a tent.'

She smiled at Sarah. 'And hope that Sarah is kind enough to keep sharing her tent with you. Which reminds me,' she said, swinging her guitar in front of her again. She began to strum tunelessly. 'It's fun to share. It's good to care. Sharing is great, so be aware . . .'

Jake forced a smile and tried his best not to groan as Lucy launched into the chorus of her next song. Maybe being dragged off by the Creeper wouldn't have been so bad after all.

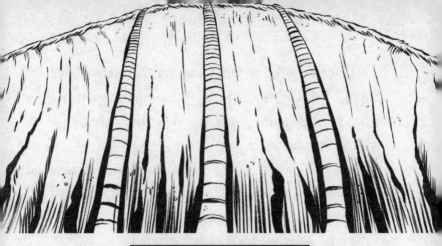

## CHAPTER SEVEN

# DeScENt INTo TeRRoR

By the time Lucy had finished her song about sharing—and another one she improvised about the importance of friendship—Jake, Sarah, and Liam only just made it to breakfast.

As it happened, they were quite relieved to miss most of breakfast, as Mr Campion had set the morning's menu, and there was nothing on offer except baked beetroot, lentil porridge, and something the head teacher insisted was toast, but was actually thinly sliced bits of sweet potato.

Luckily, Sarah had packed some bags of crisps, and, if only to avoid being sung at by Lucy again, happily shared them with the boys.

With breakfast out of the way, Jake and his friends

headed off to start the day's activity. They all groaned when they saw Callum and Matthew waiting for them.

'Fancy seeing you three here,' Callum said. 'What are the chances of us ending up in the same group *again*?'

'Pretty high, I'm guessing,' said Jake. 'You chose the same activity as us on purpose.'

Callum snorted. 'Yeah, right. Like I'd choose to hang out with you losers.'

'But you did,' said Matthew. 'Remember? You told me to find out what they were going to be doing today so we could—'

'Yes, thank you, Matthew. Shut up,' Callum said. He about-turned and marched over to where Lucy was unravelling some long lengths of rope. Matthew hesitated for a minute, then trotted after him.

'Great, another day with those two,' Jake sighed.

'Still, at least we've got Lucy today and not Terry,' said Liam.

Jake rolled his eyes. 'Go on, Sarah. Ask him who Terry is.'

Sarah frowned. 'Who's Terry?'

'That bloke,' said Liam. 'From yesterday. With the kayak.'

'You mean Dave?' said Sarah. 'His name's Dave.'

'Is it?' said Liam. 'Who's Terry, then?'

'Like I said yesterday, no idea,' said Jake. 'Anyway, Dave seemed alright.'

'Yeah, at least he didn't burst into song every five minutes,' agreed Sarah. She gestured over to Lucy, who was in the process of strapping Callum into a safety harness. 'Now, shall we?'

Twenty minutes later Jake, Liam, and Sarah stood at the top of a high cliff, their backs to the edge. They wore safety harnesses around their waists, with a long length of climbing rope threaded through a loop at the front, and hooked through a metal fastener at the back.

They were trying their best not to look scared, despite the massive drop right behind them. Jake had never been abseiling before, but it had seemed like a good idea when he'd put his name down to give it a try. Now, though, with the wind swirling around them and the ground a dizzyingly long way away, he was starting to have second thoughts.

'You look like you're about to wet yourselves,' sniggered Callum, who sat on a rock with Matthew, watching them.

'Yeah, well at least we're brave enough to go first,' said Sarah. 'Unlike you two.'

Callum let out a sharp cackle. 'It was nothing to do with bravery. I just wanted to be up here to see the terror on your faces when you went over the edge.'

Liam's head whipped round. 'Wait. What? Over the edge? What does he mean *over the edge*?' He glanced back at the drop behind them. 'We're not going down there, are we?'

'Er, yeah,' said Jake. 'That's sort of the whole point of abseiling.'

Liam's eyes widened. '*Abseiling*? I thought we were going sailing! You know, with boats and stuff.'

'Why would we be standing on top of a cliff with a rope tied round us?' Sarah asked.

'I don't know!' said Liam.

'The water is a mile and a half that way,' Jake pointed out.

'I mean, I did think that was a bit weird, but I'm not an expert, am I?' Liam protested.

Lucy approached them, her smile ramped all the way up to ten. 'Ready, guys?' she asked, giving them a double thumbs-up. 'Remember everything I showed you?'

'I don't think I can do it,' Jake admitted, much to Callum's amusement.

'Chicken!'

'Shut up, Callum,' Sarah snapped. She looked at Lucy and shook her head. 'I'm not sure I can, either.'

Lucy nodded. 'Don't worry, I thought this might happen,' she said. 'Which is why I took the liberty of composing this little number.'

She reached into her backpack and pulled out a lemon-yellow ukulele. To everyone's amazement, she played that even worse than she played the guitar. 'Frightened, frightened, frightened little mouse . . .' she began, but that was as much as Jake, Sarah, and Liam heard.

'On second thoughts, let's do this,' said Jake.

'Right behind you!' agreed Sarah.

'Don't leave me behind!' Liam yelped. Holding tightly to their ropes, they all leaned backwards and stepped out into thin air.

At first, Jake was convinced he was going to plunge towards the ground, before going *splat* against it at the bottom. Instead, though, he found himself completely supported by the rope, which he held behind him with one hand.

'That's it!' Lucy cheered. 'Feed the rope out slowly, and walk down the cliff face. That's the way!'

Jake laughed. He couldn't help it. All the panic of last night and that morning evaporated as he dangled forty metres off the ground, his feet flat against the rocky cliff. 'It's not that bad, actually,' he said, then he laughed harder when Liam bounced past him.

'It's your friendly neighbourhood Spider-Liam!' he yelled, making web-shooter sounds as he made his way down the cliff.

Sarah rolled her eyes. 'He's such an idiot,' she said, taking a few bouncing steps of her own. 'It's pretty fun, this, you know, once you get past the almost overwhelming sense of impending doom.'

They all looked up in time to see Lucy, Callum, and a very reluctant Matthew making their way over the edge on their own ropes. Liam's voice drifted up from below. 'Last one to the bottom's a rotten leg!'

Jake looked across at Sarah. They were both neck and neck on the cliff-side now. 'Does he mean rotten egg?'

Sarah shrugged. 'Your guess is as good as mine,' she said. 'Three, two, one . . . Go!'

They both kicked their legs, bouncing themselves away from the rock. Frantically, they fed the rope through their hands, lowering themselves faster and faster towards the ground below. They quickly gained on Liam, and by the time they were almost at the bottom, all three of them had drawn level.

The ground was only four or five metres below, while Lucy, Callum, and Matthew were still a good fifteen or more above. 'And who will take the victory?' asked Liam, doing his best sports commentator impression. 'In this thrilling race to the finish. It's going to be close!'

Suddenly, Jake felt his rope go slack. His jaw snapped together, rattling his teeth as the line gave an abrupt jerk. Then, with a *twang* the rope snapped, and Jake plunged towards the ground below. He landed awkwardly on the grass, toppling sideways as his legs collapsed below him.

'Hey, that's cheating!' Liam protested, but Sarah reached over and slapped him on the arm.

'He didn't do it on purpose!' she said, rappelling down. She landed beside Jake, who coughed and wheezed as he struggled to get his breath back. 'Jake? Jake, are you OK?' she asked.

Jake nodded, shakily. 'J-just a bit w-winded,' he said. 'Nothing broken.'

Liam landed beside them and held up the end of Jake's rope. 'I wouldn't say that, mate,' he said. 'You broke your rope.'

Sarah took the end of the rope from Liam and examined it. 'It doesn't look frayed,' she said. 'It looks like it's been cut.'

There was a frantic scrabbling of feet on rock, and Lucy dropped down beside them. 'Oh my goodness, oh my goodness,' she cried. 'Are you alright? Can you move?'

'Yeah,' said Jake, starting to sit up.

'STOP!' Lucy shouted, so loudly that her voice echoed off across the hills. 'You need to stay completely still. You might have broken your neck!'

'I don't think I have,' said Jake.

'You might be in shock!' Lucy continued.

Jake shook his head. 'No. I don't think so. Just a bit bruised.'

Lucy began to pace back and forth, squeezing the bridge of her nose between finger and thumb. 'Oh, this is all my fault. I should have checked the rope, but I did check the rope, but then I should have checked it more closely, only I thought I had checked it more closely,' she muttered, apparently arguing with herself. 'He could have been killed, but he wasn't, but that's not the point, he could have been, but he's fine, so it's not a problem, only the school are probably going to sue me and . . .'

She stopped pacing and gasped, her eyes like two saucer-sized circles of horror. 'The school might sue me!'

'I don't think they will,' said Jake, as Sarah and

Liam helped him to his feet.

'Really? You're not just saying that?' said Lucy. She reached into her backpack and pulled out her ukulele again. Jake, Sarah, and Liam gritted their teeth as she launched into an up-tempo number. 'I don't see the attraction . . . in taking legal action . . . It's not like I have anything to take!'

'It's fine, don't worry about it,' said Jake, clamping a hand over the instrument's strings. 'It was an accident, that was all. These things happen.'

Lucy's bottom lip wobbled, like she might burst into tears at any second. 'Yes,' she squeaked. 'Just an accident. These things happen.'

There was another scuffing of feet on stone as Callum dropped down beside them. He smirked. 'I have to say, Jake, that landing of yours was a bit *ropey*.'

Jake stepped closer and squared up to Callum. 'Did you have something to do with my rope breaking?' he demanded.

Callum looked offended. 'Jake, I can't believe you'd think such a thing,' he said. 'I'd never do anything to hurt a friend.'

'We're not your friends,' said Sarah, stepping up to join Jake.

'Yeah,' agreed Liam. 'You've only got one friend round here, Callum.'

All eyes followed Liam's finger as he pointed upwards. There, dangling upside-down on his rope several metres above them, was Matthew.

'I think I m-may have a problem,' Matthew mumbled. 'Also, I really quite urgently need the toilet.'

Jake and Callum both ignored him. Their eyes locked. Their fists clenched. Just before either of them could swing the first punch, Lucy stepped between them.

'Let's set sail on the good ship friendship,' she sang, strumming her ukulele completely out of time with the words. 'The good ship friendship, the good ship—'

There was a short, sharp scream from Matthew as he slid a few metres down the rope before his harness jerked him to a stop. He swung like the pendulum of a clock, his face a deathly shade of pale.

'W-well, the good news,' he began, 'is that I don't think I need the toilet any more . . .'

'Ahoy down there!' boomed a voice from the top of the cliff. Mr Campion leaned over the edge and gave them a wave. 'Everything OK?'

'Jake's rope snapped,' Lucy admitted.

'Oh,' said Mr Campion. 'Is he alive?'

'Yes.'

'Fully alive, or just a little bit?'

'He's fully alive,' Lucy replied.

'Good show,' called the head. 'No harm done, then. What doesn't kill you only makes you stronger and all that. Between you and me, I've always thought he's a bit of a wimp. Could do with a spot of toughening up. Carry on!'

He vanished out of sight again. Jake closed his mouth, which had dropped open while listening to the head teacher. 'He thinks I'm a wimp!'

Lucy frowned. 'Hey! That was between me and Mr Campion!'

'He literally shouted it from the top of a cliff!' Jake protested.

Lucy sniffed. She strummed her ukulele. 'I think someone needs to hear a little song I like to call *Private Conversations*,' she said, but luckily Matthew chose just that moment to slide clumsily down his rope and land with a *thud* on the grass.

Tucking the ukulele back in her backpack, Lucy took hold of one of Matthew's arms. 'Help me get him up,' she said to Callum, and the two of them half-carried, half-dragged the whimpering—and somewhat damp—Matthew towards the track leading back to camp.

Sarah, Jake, and Liam watched them go. 'You don't really think Callum cut the rope, do you?' Sarah asked, when the rest of the group were out of earshot.

'I don't know,' said Jake. 'He does like to prank us, and he seemed to find it pretty funny when I fell, but cutting my rope seems a bit too extreme, even for him. Maybe it did just snap.'

Sarah held up the end of the rope, showing that it had been neatly sliced. 'It was cut. No doubt about it,' she said.

'Well, if Callum didn't do it, who did?' Liam wondered.

All three of them looked up at the cliff face. Here and there they could see weeds growing outwards through cracks in the rock, but otherwise there was nothing that looked out of place.

'I think it's pretty obvious who did it,' said Sarah.

All three of them nodded and spoke at the same time.

'The Creeper,' said Sarah.

'The Creeper,' said Jake.

'The President of Mexico!' said Liam. He glanced at the others. 'Or the Creeper. Yeah. That makes more sense.'

Jake stared at the end of his rope again. 'First my pillow, and now this,' he muttered. 'I'm going to have to keep my wits about me, if I want to make it to the end of the week in one piece!'

# CAMP ACCIDENT REPORT

DATE: _18th July_

COMPLETED BY: _Lucy Donoghue_

DESCRIPTION OF INCIDENT:

So . . . OK. Don't go nuts here. This was probably my fault, but let me say right off that no one was actually hurt, so please don't fire me. I love this job.

Anyway, so what happened was that I had a few of the kids out abseiling with me, and, well, the thing is . . . one of the ropes broke. I know, I know, I should have checked it more carefully. I thought I did. I was sure I'd gone over them all the night before, but I guess I wasn't paying attention properly, because I'd come up with this amazing new song about abseiling that sort of goes, like, turn that frown upside down, abseiling's gonna get you down—in a good way. It's sort of got an R&B kind of rhythm to it, with like a country beat layered over the top.

Anyway, the point is that one of the kids, Jake Latchford, kind of plunged several metres down the cliff face before landing in a heap at the bottom. Like I say, though, he's absolutely fine. No bruises, no broken bones, no devastating spinal trauma (which was my first thought when I saw him plummeting helplessly towards the ground, to be honest).

So, I'm no scientist or anything, but I'd say that the rope must have been faulty, because I'm 99% sure that I carried out all the required safety checks on the ropes the night before. Or, you know, 95% sure, anyway.

85% sure at the absolute minimum.

I'll keep an eye on him to make sure his legs don't stop working or anything, but I think he'll be fine.

# Lucy xx

PS—Oh, and another boy fell off, too, but that was his own fault and nothing to do with me.

Was rope frayed or cut, like Jake suggested? Report doesn't state.

## CHAPTER EIGHT

# CREEPING AROUND

Jake spent the rest of the day in a state of high alert, jumping whenever anyone made any sudden movements, and keeping as far from trees, shrubs, and other foliage as possible. Considering the camp was completely surrounded by the stuff, that wasn't easy.

That evening, he skipped out of the campfire ghost story session, on the basis that he'd had quite enough scares for one day, thanks very much, and that after the excitement of his near-death experience, he could do with an early night.

'I'm sure you two are tired, too,' he said, shooting Liam and Sarah a meaningful look.

'Not particularly,' said Liam, chomping on a hot dog that had been cooked in the smoke of the fire.

'I slept like a log last night.'

'You sure?' said Jake, nodding slowly. 'You look tired. Maybe you should get an early night, too.'

'Nah, we're fine,' said Sarah.

'I'm *too* awake, if anything,' said Liam.

Jake glanced very deliberately towards the tent. 'No . . . think about it. Listen to what I'm saying,' he urged. 'You look tired. Maybe we—all three of us—should leave the campfire where everyone else is, and go to the tent.'

'What's the matter, Jake? You too scared to be on your own?' snorted Callum.

'Man up, lad!' barked Mr Campion. 'If you're tired, take yourself off to your tent, but don't drag your friends along to hold your hand.'

Sarah swallowed her burger. 'Maybe Jake's right,' she told Liam. 'We should go.'

'Nonsense!' said Mr Campion. 'Jake, off you trot. You two, stay right where you are, and let me tell you a terrifying tale about a monster they call . . . childhood obesity!'

An hour later, Liam and Sarah climbed into the

**71**

tent. Jake sat on top of his sleeping bag, a heavy stick clutched in both hands like a club. He let out a sigh of relief when he saw his friends, and lowered the weapon.

'What took you so long?' he asked.

'It was Mr Campion's story,' Sarah said. 'He literally listed every junk food known to man.'

'It made me so hungry!' Liam groaned, rubbing his rumbling stomach. 'Which I think was probably the opposite effect to the one he was hoping for.'

'Anyway, what's up?' asked Sarah.

Jake sighed. 'It's too late now. I thought that when everyone was gathered at the campfire, we could have snuck into the camp office and looked for clues.'

'Brilliant idea!' cried Liam. He frowned. 'Clues to what?'

'To what happened to my rope,' said Jake.

'I thought the Creeper did it?' said Liam.

Jake shifted uncomfortably. 'Well, yeah. I mean. . . probably. But I want to know for sure. Maybe it was just an accident, or maybe Callum did it. It might even have been Lucy!'

Liam drew in a sharp breath. 'How *dare* you, sir? That's my future wife you're talking about!'

'Why would Lucy try to kill you?' Sarah wondered.

'He can be quite annoying sometimes,' said Liam,

shrugging. 'No offence.'

'Loads taken!' said Jake. He shook his head. 'She probably didn't. But it's worth having a look, isn't it? We have to do something, otherwise it feels like I'm just sitting around waiting for the Creeper to finish me off.'

'Still,' said Liam. 'At least he only seems to be going for you, so that's a bit of a relief.'

Jake and Sarah both glared at him. Liam blinked. 'What?'

Sarah shook her head. 'You really are unbelievable sometimes!'

'I'm just saying, at least he's only going for one of us, and not trying to kill all three of us,' Liam said. 'It's a bit of a silver lining, that's all.'

'Unless he wants to get rid of us one at a time,' said Jake. 'And he's saving you for last.'

Liam swallowed. 'What? Why would he do that?'

'You're the one who led all the potato-men to their doom,' Jake pointed out.

Liam's jaw dropped. 'You're right, that was me.'

'You turned them all into lumpy mash,' Jake continued.

'I did!' Liam whimpered. 'I did do that!' He hurriedly pulled the zip of the tent closed and grabbed for Jake's stick. 'We've got to get to the bottom of this,' he said. 'We've got to find out what the Creeper is up to, and stop him!'

Sarah nodded. 'We should sleep in shifts,' she said. 'Make sure he doesn't come for Jake—or any of us—during the night.'

Liam clutched the stick tightly to his chest. 'I'll take first watch,' he said. 'I'm more awake than you two.'

Jake and Sarah climbed into their sleeping bags. 'You sure?' Jake asked.

'Oh yes,' said Liam, setting his jaw in determination. 'Nothing will get past me, don't you worry.'

He settled back against the side of the tent. He fixed his eyes on the door at the far end.

Then, almost immediately, he fell fast asleep.

'I've got a bobsleigh made of biscuits,' he mumbled, as he began to snore.

Sarah sighed and plucked the stick from her brother's hands. 'On second thoughts,' she said. 'Maybe I should take first watch.'

'It's fine, I'll stay up,' said Jake, settling down in his sleeping bag. 'I don't think I'll be able to get to sleep, anyway.'

Jake jumped awake. A terrible din vibrated the canvas walls of the tent. It sounded like a herd of screaming elephants being squeezed under a steamroller, but Liam somehow managed to sleep right through it.

'What is that?' Sarah yelled, clamping her hands over her ears.

'I have no idea!' Jake shouted. 'But I'm guessing it's nothing good!'

Sarah pulled up the door zip and they both poked their heads out. Mr Campion was standing just a few metres from the tent, blowing into a battered old trumpet. His face was red and his eyes bulged from the effort as he wheezed his way through the final few notes.

'Good morning, campers!' he cried, once the tune—if, indeed, it could be called a tune—was over. All around the camp, bleary-eyed faces glared out from their tents, trying to figure out just what was going on.

'What time is it?' asked a girl whose hair seemed to be standing straight upwards.

'It's the best time of day!' Mr Campion cried.

Liam's head popped out between Sarah and Jake's. 'Lunchtime?' he guessed, excitedly.

'Better!' said the head teacher.

'Dinner time?' said Liam.

'Even better. It's 5 *a.m.*!'

Liam's lips moved silently, as he tried to figure out the meaning of those words. 'Like . . . in the morning?' he said.

'Yes!' said Mr Campion.

'5 *a.m. in the morning*?' Liam said. 'Is that a real thing? That's not . . . that's not an actual time, is it?'

'Of course!'

'That's an actual real time that exists on the real clock?'

A flicker of irritation passed across Mr Campion's face. 'Yes! Now everyone get up, we've got a fun-packed day of gruelling hard work ahead of us!'

One big groan seemed to ripple around the camp.

'But first . . .' Mr Campion cried, reaching into a bag and pulling out several large radishes and what might have been a turnip, but which might equally have been an oddly-shaped rock. 'Breakfast!'

As they'd eaten all Sarah's crisps the day before, Jake and his friends had no choice but to force down some of Mr Campion's breakfast vegetables. By the time they had finished, Jake still couldn't say with any absolute certainty whether the thing the head teacher had held up was a turnip or a rock. Judging by the effort it had taken to bite through, though, he would probably guess 'rock'.

After breakfast, Mr Campion made everyone copy him as he did more jumping jacks than any of the pupils thought was humanly possible. By the time 6 a.m. rolled around, pretty much everyone was ready to collapse back into their sleeping bags again, and snooze the day away.

Mr Campion, though, had other ideas.

'It's Dave's day off today, so I'll be leading us on a vigorous forest walk!' he announced. 'Be aware, the pace will be fast, the terrain will be rough, and dilly-dallying will not be tolerated!'

'Sounds like a barrel of laughs,' Liam muttered.

'Do we all have to go, sir?' asked Callum. Jake was pleased to see that he looked as miserable and exhausted as everyone else.

'Indeed you do!' said Mr Campion. 'It's compulsory. But don't worry, we've come up with a way to make it extra fun!'

From over on the left came a piercing blast on a mouth organ. Lucy joined Mr Campion, as he ordered everyone to fall into step behind him.

'We are walking in a line!' Lucy sang, although that was a generous description of the noise she actually made.

'Everyone!' Mr Campion cheered.

'We are walking in a line,' mumbled the group,

**77**

trudging sleepily along behind Lucy and the head teacher.

'5 a.m.'s a feel-good time!' Lucy warbled.

Liam yawned. 'D'you know what? I'm really starting to go off her,' he muttered.

'This is great,' Jake whispered.

Liam and Sarah both looked at him in surprise. 'No it isn't,' said Liam. 'It's literally the worst thing to have ever happened in the world ever. They made us eat radishes, Jake. *Radishes*. I didn't even know that was a food.' He shook his head, remembering the taste. 'In fact, I'm still not convinced it is.'

'No, I meant it's great that everyone's leaving the camp. We can sneak back in a while and check the place over.'

'For clues!' Sarah realized.

'Exactly. If everyone's out of the camp, we'll have free rein to search the place,' said Jake. 'If there's any evidence about the Creeper, or about what happened to my rope, then we'll find it.'

'Louder at the back!' bellowed Mr Campion.

Jake, Sarah, and Liam all sighed. 'Forest hikes are lots of fun!' they sang. 'Be careful just to walk, not run.'

Two miles and twenty-seven whole verses later, Mr Campion led the conga-line of campers onto a narrow track leading down to the side of the lake. 'Just another ten miles or so,' he announced. 'Then we can have a five minute rest!'

Jake caught Sarah and Liam by their sleeves and held them back. Ahead of them, the rest of the class filed onto the path and down the hillside towards the lake. When he was sure no one had spotted them, Jake led his friends back in the direction of the forest.

'Now's our chance,' he said.

They slipped through a gap in the trees and tucked themselves in behind a thick, prickly bush. They lurked there for a few minutes, listening as the voices of Lucy and the other campers grew fainter, then finally became too far away to hear.

'OK, let's go,' said Jake, taking a few steps into the woods.

'Um . . . shouldn't we stick to the path?' Liam asked. 'It's pretty dark in here.'

'No time,' said Jake. 'We need to get back, search the camp, then try to catch up with the others before they notice we're gone.'

They all glanced around them at the towering trees. The dense leaves hung like a canopy above them, blocking out most of the sky. 'I don't like it either,' Jake said. 'But if we go the long way we'll never catch up. This is our only option.'

Reluctantly, Liam and Sarah agreed that taking a shortcut through the woods was the best plan. That didn't mean they had to like it, though, and Liam spent most of the next twenty minutes grumbling about tripping on roots, and squealing in panic when anything moved in the trees.

'What was that one?' he shrieked, as something hopped between two branches ahead of them.

'Chaffinch, I think,' Sarah sighed.

Liam stared anxiously at the little bird. 'Could it be a killer chaffinch?'

'I doubt it,' Sarah said.

They weaved on through the woods, clambering over small clumps of shrubs and bushes, and picking a path around the larger ones. The deeper they got into the woods, the thicker the foliage became. Soon, almost all of the morning sunlight had been blocked by the tangled branches, and Jake found himself stumbling through shadows.

'Is it my imagination . . .?' said Liam.

'Probably,' said Sarah.

'Or are the trees looking . . . angrier?'

Sarah snorted. 'Angrier? What do you mean? How can the trees look . . .?'

She stopped talking when she looked at the trees around them. She couldn't explain how, exactly, but

Liam was right. There was something about the trees which made them look far meaner and more sinister than they had just a few moments ago.

'Those branches do seem to be getting closer,' Sarah said, gesturing to where a claw-like spray of pointed twigs appeared to be reaching out for Jake.

Jake ducked under the branch and held his breath, waiting for it to make a grab for him. Instead, it just let out a low *creak* and bent gently upwards towards the sky.

'Just the wind,' he said. 'That's all. Nothing to worry about.'

Sarah caught him by the arm and pulled him back. 'What about that?' she whispered, pointing through a gap in some trees ahead.

There, right ahead of them, was the creepy abandoned tent Callum had led them to on the first day. Only by the looks of things, it wasn't abandoned any more. A shape moved around inside the tent, making the mouldy canvas sides shudder and bulge.

'There's something in there,' Sarah said.

'Or some*thing*,' whispered Liam.

'That's what I just said,' Sarah hissed.

'Oh, was it?' Liam replied. 'I'll be honest, I was only half-listening.'

They all ducked down behind a knot of bushes

and watched the tent. 'Do you think it's the Creeper?' Sarah asked.

'I sort of hope it is,' said Liam. The others looked at him in surprise. 'Well, think about it—either it's an evil half-man, half-plant monster, or it's some crazy weirdo who lives in a manky tent miles from anywhere. At least if it's the Creeper we know what we're dealing with.'

Jake opened his mouth to argue, but then closed it again. Liam had a point. 'Better the devil you know than the devil you don't, I suppose,' Jake admitted.

'Should we rush the tent, do you think?' asked Sarah. 'Trap him inside?'

Jake and Liam both nodded slowly. 'Well, I mean we *could* do that,' said Jake.

'Yeah, we definitely *could* do that,' agreed Liam.

'But how about we just sneak round it instead, and hope he doesn't hear us?' Jake suggested.

Liam nodded. 'I very much approve of that plan. Sarah?'

Sarah looked positively relieved. 'Yep. Works for me,' she whispered.

Slowly, carefully, they crept out from behind the bushes and tiptoed their way through the trees. The gnarled branches and overgrown undergrowth meant the only route they could take brought them worryingly close to the spot where the tent stood.

'Easy,' Jake whispered. The tent was just a few metres away now, and whatever was in there seemed to be getting agitated. Jake had hoped it might turn out to be a fox or something, but it was easily human-sized, and possibly even bigger.

'Why couldn't we just have gone on Mr Campion's nice walk?' Liam whimpered. 'A brisk twenty-mile hike sounds like a lot of fun right now!'

'Shh!' Sarah urged. 'We don't want him to hear us.'

The tent shook violently, making all three of them jump. There was a *snap* as one of the poles inside broke in two, and a *rrrip* as something tore through the ancient canvas.

A twisted, branch-like arm forced its way out through the hole, followed by the top of a leafy green head. Two glowing eyes glared at them.

'Well, well, well,' hissed the terrifying figure. 'Look who we have here.'

'It's him! It's the Creeper!' Jake cried. 'Run for it!'

## CHAPTER NINE

# HUNTED!

Jake, Sarah, and Liam crashed through the forest, leaping and bounding over roots, and ducking low limbs. As they ran, the woods seemed to come alive around them, the branches squeezing together, trying to slow them down.

'Is he coming?' Sarah yelped. 'Can anyone see him?'

'Don't know, don't care!' Jake cried. 'Just keep running!'

The camp lay just a few dozen metres ahead. They could see a few of the tents through the gaps in the tree trunks, but those gaps were growing narrower, as if the tree trunks were growing wider, forming one big solid wall.

'Hurry!' Jake urged. The spaces between the trunks

were barely big enough for them to fit through now. Lowering their heads, they each picked a different gap and powered towards it. With three grunts of effort, they all launched themselves through the narrowing spaces.

Thin branches scrabbled at their legs, trying to snare them, but then they were through the gaps, out of the woods . . . and heading face-first for an enormous puddle of mud.

SPLUT!

All three of them flopped into the gooey brown sludge, splattering themselves from head to toe. The mud sloshed as they spun around, expecting to see a wall of wood. But the trees looked just like trees, and the gaps between them were as wide as they ever were.

'But . . . but . . .' Liam began. He glanced at the others. 'Did anyone else think the trees were moving, or was it just me?'

'They were,' Jake panted. 'They definitely were, I'm sure of it.' They both turned to Sarah. 'I mean . . . right?'

Sarah nodded, but slowly. 'I . . . I mean, I thought so, but maybe we were imagining it?'

'What, all of us?' said Jake. 'At the same time?'

'It's happened before,' said Liam, pulling himself up out of the mud with a series of squelching fart noises he'd normally have found hilarious, but which he was still far too terrified to laugh about. 'Remember that time we imagined the school football field got dug up to plant potatoes?'

Jake blinked. 'That actually happened.'

Liam frowned. 'What?'

'We didn't imagine that,' said Jake, getting to his feet. 'That actually did happen.'

'Did it?' said Liam.

'Yes!' said Sarah, pulling herself free of muddy sludge.

'Oh,' said Liam. 'Well . . . OK, then. That actually explains a lot.'

Jake took a few steps closer to the edge of the forest and peered into the shadows. If the trees had been moving, they were back to normal now. There was no sign that anything had been chasing them, so either they'd lost the Creeper somewhere in the woods, or they'd all imagined him, too.

A vision of the terrifying figure forcing its way out from inside the tent reared up in Jake's head. He shuddered. There was no way his imagination was that good.

Giving himself a shake, he turned back to the matter at hand. 'Right, we need to search this place from top to bottom,' he said.

'What are we looking for, specifically?' asked Liam.

'Clues,' said Jake.

'Can you be more specific than that?' Liam said.

Jake shrugged. 'I don't know. Just . . . stuff.'

'That's less specific, if anything,' Liam pointed out.

Jake sighed. 'I don't know what we're looking for, just anything out of the ordinary. I'll know it when I see it.'

'So, like a big knife that could be used for cutting an abseiling rope, for example?' said Sarah.

'Exactly!'

Sarah reached into the nearest tent. 'Like this one, you mean?' she said, holding up a large, deadly-looking survival knife. She peered at it more closely, then plucked a single strand of fibre from a notch where the blade met the handle.

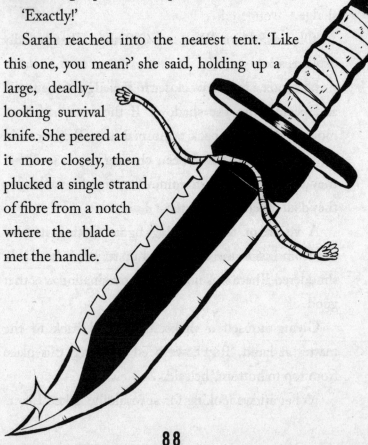

'Blue rope,' said Sarah. 'Like yours.'

Jake took the strand and studied it. 'You're right. This is just like mine. Whose tent is this?'

Liam squatted down and reached inside. His heart sank when he pulled out a brightly-coloured acoustic guitar. 'Oh, great,' he sighed. 'My future wife wants to kill my best friend. That puts me in a bit of an awkward position.'

'I don't understand. Why would Lucy want to kill me?' Jake wondered.

Liam puffed out his cheeks. 'Dunno. Maybe she just wanted to get you out of the way so she'd have me all to herself.' He looked across at his sister. 'She'll probably go after you next.'

Sarah tossed the knife back inside the tent. 'Or maybe it's coincidence. She's a camp leader. She probably cuts ropes all the time.'

Liam gasped. 'She's a mass-murderer?'

'No! I mean she probably has to cut them to the right length for people to use and stuff, not that she's going round hacking up everyone's rope when they're using it.'

Jake pointed to the strap of the guitar. The rainbow design had been replaced by a length of blue rope. 'Or she might have used it to make a new guitar strap.'

Sarah nodded. 'Ah. Yes. That would do it.'

Liam glanced from Jake to Sarah and back again. 'So . . . what are we saying? She's not a crazy serial killer?'

'Probably not,' said Jake.

'Phew!' Liam laughed. 'Well that's a relief. Now all we need to do is get her to stop singing and—'

There was an angry hiss and a sudden rustle of foliage right behind them. Squealing in panic, Liam spun on the spot, swinging the guitar in a wide, sweeping arc.

The noise the instrument made as it whanged against the hulking figure behind them was not pleasant, but probably wasn't the worst sound to ever come out of it. The wood splintered into pieces, the strings twanging as they snapped in two.

Jake, Sarah, and Liam all watched in horror as the man whose head Liam had just smashed the guitar over flopped face-first into the mud.

'Terry!' Liam gasped. 'I killed Terry.'

'Dave,' corrected Jake.

'Dave, right, yeah,' said Liam. He frowned. 'So, who's—'

'We don't know who Terry is!' Sarah snapped.

They stared down at the unmoving Dave. 'Is he dead?' Liam asked.

'I don't know,' said Jake. 'Check his pulse.'

'You check his pulse!' Liam replied.

'Why should I do it? I didn't hit him with a guitar!'

Sarah tutted. 'I'll do it,' she said, but as she bent down Dave let out a loud groan. They all jumped back in fright.

'Well?' hissed Liam, once his heart had slowed from machine-gun speeds. 'Are you going to check his pulse or what?'

Sarah rolled her eyes. 'Give me strength!' she muttered. 'No. He just made a noise. He's clearly alive.'

'Right, yeah, good point,' Liam said. They all stared down at Dave, lying unconscious face-down in the mud. 'Think he'll be mad?' asked Liam.

'Well, I doubt he'll be grateful,' said Jake. 'Come on, we'd better get him up.'

Jake reached down, then screamed when Dave's hand shot up and caught him by the front of his t-shirt. Dave lifted his head, his mud-splattered face twisting into a furious snarl.

'What are you doing here?' he demanded.

'W-we got lost,' Jake stammered. 'We wandered off from the rest of the group, s-so we headed back here.'

Dave's eyes narrowed, but he released his grip and jumped to his feet in one bounding leap. Gingerly, he rubbed his head where the guitar had hit him. 'I told you on the first day, you don't go wandering in the woods,' Dave said. 'It was one of the first rules.'

'We know,' said Sarah. 'And we're sorry. We just fell behind and thought it safer to come back here than to keep searching for the rest of the group. We remember what you said about safety being so important.'

'*So* important,' agreed Jake. 'We really took your talk to heart.'

'It was the most powerfully moving speech we ever heard,' added Liam, taking things too far as usual. 'Beautiful, really. I was crying at one point.'

Dave grunted and scooped some of the mud from his face. He gestured down at the broken instrument in Liam's hand. 'You broke Lucy's guitar.'

Liam pointlessly tried to hide the shattered wood behind his back. 'Um . . . no I didn't.'

'Yes, he did,' said Sarah.

Liam shot her an accusing look. 'Well, thanks a lot.'

Dave shrugged. 'Forget it. At least some good came of this. Now, if we could only get rid of her ukulele, too . . .'

Jake, Sarah, and Liam all started to laugh, then stopped when Dave flashed them a furious look.

'Don't think everything's fine and we're all friends again,' he warned.

He began advancing, and the children all found themselves backing away. 'You deliberately disobeyed the rules. You went poking around in other people's things. You hit me over the head with a guitar,' Dave said, his voice a menacing growl.

'It does sound pretty bad when you say it in a list like that,' Liam babbled.

He and the others had backed all the way up to the toilet block now. They stopped with their backs pressed against the wood. Dave continued to advance on them.

'What are you going to do to us?' Jake asked.

'Something I should have done the moment I set eyes on you,' Dave said.

'Ahoy there!'

Jake, Sarah, and Liam turned to see Mr Campion striding into the camp, carrying Matthew over one shoulder. The rest of the class trudged along behind him, all looking red-faced and exhausted.

'This clumsy oaf went over his ankle, thought I'd best bring him back to camp!'

Dave ignored the head and leaned right in so his face was just a few centimetres from Jake's. 'I'm going to be keeping a very close eye on you three,' he warned. 'Whatever you do . . . whatever mischief you might think about getting up to, I'll be watching. Got it?'

They all nodded frantically. 'Got it,' Jake whispered.

Dave smiled and clapped him on the shoulder. 'Good. Now off you go. I can't wait to see you explain all this to Mr Campion. I hear he can be very creative with his punishments . . .'

Several long hours of peeling potatoes and scrubbing the toilet blocks later, Jake, Sarah, and Liam flopped into their sleeping bags.

'You know,' said Sarah, 'after the Creeper's army of spud-people, I really thought I couldn't hate potatoes any more than I already did. After today, though, I realize I was wrong. I mean . . . how many potatoes does he think we're going to eat? We'd need to scoff about a thousand each to justify all those.'

'Peeling all those spuds was pretty terrible,' Liam groaned. 'But cleaning the toilets with our toothbrushes was far worse.'

Jake and Sarah both lifted their heads to look at him. 'What?' said Jake. 'We didn't have to use our toothbrushes.'

Liam frowned. 'Didn't we?'

'No!' said Sarah. 'Mr Campion gave us all those scrubbing brushes and cleaning products!'

'Oh. Right. So . . . were we supposed to use those?' Liam asked.

'Of course we were!' said Jake.

'Wait, wait, wait,' Sarah began. 'You didn't use your toothbrush to brush your teeth tonight, did you?'

'No, of course not!' said Liam. 'I used yours.'

Sarah twisted her face and stuck out her tongue. 'Yuck! That's disgusting! I can't believe you brushed your teeth with my toothbrush.'

'No, I didn't. I meant I used your toothbrush to clean the toilets,' Liam said. He grinned when he saw the look of sheer horror on his sister's face. 'Just kidding, just kidding!'

They all settled back. Lucy had taken pity on Jake and given him one of the camp's spare pillows, on the understanding he didn't impale this one on a branch. Jake had promised to do his best.

'I can't believe Dave caught us,' said Sarah.

'Which one's Dave again? Is he Terry's mate?' asked Liam, but the others decided just to ignore him.

'What was he even doing here?' Jake wondered. 'He was supposed to have the day off.'

Sarah shrugged. 'No idea.'

'That's the problem, we've got no idea about

anything,' Jake said with a sigh. 'We don't know where the Creeper went, we don't know for sure that it was him who cut my rope—we don't know anything.'

'We do,' said Sarah. 'We know what the Creeper looks like in human form, so at least he can't ambush us.'

'Yeah, if he wants to be sneaky he'll have to get the trees to strangle us, or have branches stab us through the head like they tried to do to Jake before.'

Jake stared up at the canvas ceiling. 'Well, that's a comforting thought,' he said. 'Thanks for that.'

All three of them yawned at the same time. Jake knew one of them should stand guard, but they were all exhausted after their day of chores, and no matter how hard they tried, none of them could stop their eyelids fluttering closed, as they all fell into a deep, soundless sleep.

'I never want to be a sandwich,' said Liam, tossing and turning fitfully in his sleeping bag. 'Don't pop me like a pimple!'

Jake forced an eye open. It blinked several times as it tried to adjust to the midnight gloom, then swivelled to fix on Liam. He was close. Much closer than he had been when they'd all gone to sleep.

Sarah was close to Liam on the other side, too, bunched up tight between her brother and the tent's canvas wall.

Jake's sleep-fuzzed brain tried to process this information. The wall he was closest to was pressing against him, and yet he seemed to be nearer the middle than he'd been earlier. Which meant . . .

What? His brain still wasn't firing on all cylinders, and nothing was making sense. He forced open his other eye to see if that would help somehow.

'The tent's smaller,' he mumbled. That was it. The tent had shrunk in the night, forcing him closer to Jake and Sarah.

Satisfied he'd figured it out, Jake closed his eyes and began to drift off again.

Something screamed at him from the very back of his brain. He tried to ignore it. He was so tired, and whatever it was could wait until morning, he was sure.

But the screaming continued, alerting him to the massive, gaping flaw in his thinking.

Jake's eyes flicked open, both at once this time. 'How can the tent be smaller?' he said, loud enough this time to wake up Sarah. She sat upright, only to find the tent wall pressing down on her.

'What's going on?' she gasped.

'The tent's got smaller,' Jake told her.

'How can the tent have got smaller?'

'It can't,' said Jake, his voice a whisper. 'I think . . . I think something's squeezing it from outside.'

As if on cue, the tent's poles groaned and the space inside tightened around them even further. The whole construction lurched sideways. Sarah screamed as she was thrown on top of her brother. Liam didn't stir, other than to let out a single loud snore.

'We're going to be crushed!' Jake yelped, scrabbling out of his bag and crawling to the door. He grabbed the zip and pulled, but something on the other side held it tightly in place. 'It's stuck! I can't get it open!'

Sarah appeared beside him. They both caught the little loop of cord attached to the zip and heaved together. The zip crept open a centimetre or so, and they both leaped back as a narrow vine twisted into the gap in the door.

They watched in wonder as the vine snaked through the zip, snapped the metal fastener off, then retreated outside again. A moment later, the zip was closed from the outside.

'D-did you see that?' Sarah yelped.

Jake nodded, then ducked as the walls of the tent crushed closer. 'It's the Creeper. He's trying to squash us!' Jake realized. He tried to push back against the walls, but the vines had completely cocooned the tent on all sides, and it was like trying to fight the forest itself.

'Help!' Sarah screamed. 'Help us!'

'Someone help!' Jake yelped, but both their voices sounded muffled by the prison of vines.

'I don't think anyone can hear us,' Sarah realized.

'Space jockeys need kittens, too,' Liam mumbled.

'Unbelievable!' Jake said. 'He really can sleep through anything.'

The tent lurched again, and Jake and Sarah were both thrown off balance. They felt a bumping and thudding below them, heard the low hissing and rumbling of the tent being pulled along the ground.

They realized at the same time what was happening. The Creeper was dragging their tent out of the camp. He was stealing them away in the dead of night.

And there was no way for them to escape.

## CHAPTER TEN

# THE MONSTER STRIKES

The dragging went on for so long, Jake and Sarah began to feel travel sick. They screamed and hollered as they were flung around like ragdolls inside the tent, all the while trying very hard not to throw up. Liam, for his part, kept snoring and occasionally shouted stuff about fish fingers and flying monkeys.

'Where is he taking us?' Sarah yelped, as they bounced into the air then landed hard on the floor again.

'Somewhere nice, hopefully,' said Jake. 'I hear the Lake District is lovely at this time of year.'

'I somehow doubt he's taking us on holiday,' Sarah replied.

'Let's see if he likes *this*,' said Jake. Laying back, he

kicked against one of the walls with both feet, but the vines just tightened their grip, narrowing the space even further. 'On second thoughts,' Jake mumbled. 'That was possibly a mistake.'

On and on the lurching went, the rumbling of the uneven ground beneath them eventually becoming a steady roaring hiss. They were being dragged across grass, Jake guessed, but he couldn't be sure.

And then, without warning, the noise and the movement both stopped. A still silence fell over the tent. Jake and Sarah both held their breath. Waiting. Listening. But there wasn't a single sound to be heard other than the distant rustling of leaves on the breeze, and the faint buzzing of a bee somewhere not too far away.

'Wassat?' cried Liam, sitting bolt-upright. His head clonked hard against Jake's and Sarah's. They all clutched their skulls and groaned in pain.

'Ow!' Jake groaned.

'Watch it,' said Sarah.

Liam glared accusingly at them both. 'What you doing leaning over me?' he demanded. 'Have you been drawing on my face? Have I got a felt tip moustache?'

Jake shook his head. 'No.'

Liam looked crestfallen. 'Oh. I've always wanted a felt tip moustache.' His eyes darted across the walls and ceiling. 'Here, how come everything's so small? Have you moved me to a different tent again?'

Jake and Sarah both shook their heads. 'It's the Creeper,' Sarah whispered.

Liam frowned. 'The Creeper moved me to a different tent? Why did he do that?'

Before anyone could answer, there was a loud *zzzzzip* as the tent door was pulled open. Half a dozen vines reached inside, holding the door flaps apart.

'I think that's an invitation to go outside,' said Jake.

Liam clutched the edges of his sleeping bag. 'Can we politely decline?'

Another vine stretched inside and made a series of beckoning motions. 'I'd reckon that's probably a "no",' said Sarah.

'Stick together,' Jake whispered. 'But if you see a chance to make a run back to camp, do it. Agreed?'

'OK.' Sarah nodded.

'Got it,' said Liam, slipping out of his sleeping bag.

Jake smiled grimly. 'Right then, let's go and see what's out there.'

They clambered out, Jake leading the way, with Sarah and Liam following close behind. The forest surrounded them on all sides, looking deeper and darker than ever before. And there, slouching in front of them, was the abandoned tent.

The mould-patterned walls were ripped and torn, giving them a glimpse of something moving inside.

Liam let out a sudden gasp. 'I've just had a terrible thought,' he whispered. 'What if that's the Creeper in there?'

Sarah rolled her eyes. 'Well, *of course* it's the Creeper. Who else could it be?'

The tent flap was thrown back. A figure emerged.

'Er . . . it's not the Creeper,' said Jake.

'Callum?!' said Liam. 'Callum's the bad guy? Well, I did *not* see that coming.'

'I don't think so,' Sarah whispered. 'Look at him.'

Callum's eyes were wide and staring, his face a mess of snot and tears. Vines were wrapped around him, pinning his arms to his sides.

'H-help me!' he sobbed, but then the vines twisted across his mouth, stopping him saying any more. He tumbled to the ground, the foliage tangling around his legs. Jake moved to help him, but a sharp, sudden bark from inside the tent made him stop.

'Leave him!'

'This'll be the Creeper,' whispered Liam. 'Bet you anything. This'll definitely be the Creeper.'

Another, much larger figure emerged from inside the tent. To everyone's surprise, this one wasn't the Creeper, either.

'Dave?' said Jake.

'Dave!' said Sarah.

'*Terry?*' said Liam.

'What's going on?' Jake demanded. 'What have you done to Callum?'

Dave shrugged. 'Not my fault. He came wandering around, planning to set up another of his stupid, juvenile pranks to try to make you three look like idiots. You should be thanking me, really. You should have seen his face when he found me in there. It was a picture.'

Jake, Liam, and Sarah looked down at Callum, still struggling against the vines. 'But . . . I don't understand,' said Sarah.

'It's not difficult,' Dave snapped. 'It's in the rules. "Don't wander off." He wandered off, just like you three. How difficult is it to follow one simple rule?'

'But—'

'That's the problem with you kids nowadays,' Dave said, raising his voice. 'You don't do as you're told. You don't follow the rules!'

Jake glanced anxiously into the woods around them. 'Look, Dave, this is all really important stuff, I'm sure, but we have to get out of here.'

Dave frowned. 'Why?'

'Someone's coming,' said Sarah.

'More like some*thing*, actually,' added Liam.

'It's a monster,' Jake explained. 'It's called the Creeper.'

Dave's frown deepened. 'A monster?'

'That's right,' said Sarah, her eyes flicking from shadow to shadow. 'It dragged our tent here and—'

'Do you know,' said Dave, cutting her off, 'there are certain types of plant which are often thought of as monsters?'

He tucked his hands behind his back and began pacing back and forth, like a teacher addressing an unruly class.

'*Nepenthes rafflesiana*, for example. Found in Borneo, among other places. Its leaves are like sword blades, but that's not the interesting part,' Dave explained. 'See, these plants—a type of creeper vine, actually—they're carnivorous. Flesh-eating.'

Dave lunged forwards and chomped his teeth together, making the children all jump in fright.

'And you might think, *so what*? There are loads of plants that eat insects, right?' Dave said, his voice now a low whisper. 'Only the *Nepenthes rafflesiana* doesn't just eat bugs. It eats rats. Nosy little rats who go sticking their little ratty noses into things that aren't their business. Who go *interfering* in things that don't concern them. It swallows them whole. It

**105**

digests them alive.'

Dave paused to let that sink in for a moment. 'Incredible, isn't it?'

'Not if you're the rat,' said Liam.

Dave's face twisted slowly into a grin. 'Yes,' he said. 'Believe me, you really don't want to be the rat.'

'Look, Dave, this is all fascinating stuff, but we have to get out of here,' said Jake.

Dave either wasn't listening, or didn't care. He resumed pacing and carried on delivering his lesson.

'*Dionaea muscipula*,' he said, rolling the words theatrically around in his mouth. 'Better known as the Venus flytrap, although that hardly does it justice. Like our friend the *Nepenthes rafflesiana*, it doesn't just eat flies, but enjoys tucking into any small mammal stupid enough to wander too close. Young ones, in particular.'

Dave placed the heels of his hands together, his fingers curved so they resembled a Venus flytrap. 'It's covered in fine hairs which can detect if something is alive or dead. If it's dead, it isn't interested, but if something alive brushes against those hairs . . . SNAP!'

He slapped his hands together right in front of Jake's face. 'It shuts its jaws and seals them closed. And whatever's trapped inside is slowly dissolved.

Sometimes, it can take days. Weeks, even.'

He tucked his hands behind his back again and rocked on his heels. 'My point is, plants are incredible,' Dave said. 'Truly amazing. They can do things we can only dream of.'

'Anyone can eat flies,' said Liam. 'I mean, we've all done it.'

'Speak for yourself,' said Sarah.

'I'm sure he doesn't mean on purpose,' said Jake. He shot Liam a doubting look. 'You don't mean on purpose, do you?'

'What? Um, no,' said Liam, smiling a little too broadly. 'Definitely not, no. As if I'd ever eat flies on purpose just to see what they tasted like!'

Dave glared at them and tapped his foot, impatiently. 'Are you quite finished?' he asked. When they all nodded, he continued. 'As I was saying, plants can do things we can only dream of. Cut one back to its very roots and it will regrow. Plant them in the most inhospitable conditions, and they will still find a way to take root.'

'Yeah, great,' said Jake. 'Now, we really need to—'

'And then,' said Dave, holding up a hand for silence, 'we come to *Boquila trifoliolata*.'

'Did he say something about "trifle"?' asked Liam. 'I'd love a bit of trifle.'

'*Boquila trifoliolata* is a vine, and is without question the world's second greatest master of disguise,' said Dave. 'Able to mimic other plants perfectly, altering its shape, size, colour, and even vein patterns to be completely indistinguishable from the original. If it grows across two trees, it can mimic both at the same time. If you didn't know what you were looking for, you'd never even know it was there.'

'Impressive,' said Sarah. 'So . . . how come it's only the second greatest master of disguise?'

'Yeah,' said Liam. 'If that's second, what's the best?'

Dave's mouth turned upwards into an impossibly wide grin. 'Me,' he said, then he bent forwards and let out a deep, rumbling laugh as something heaved and squirmed beneath his staff t-shirt.

They shot each other nervous glances. All except Callum, that is, who was still face-down on the ground and couldn't really look at anyone or do very much at all.

'You alright, Terry?' asked Liam.

'Dave,' said Jake, automatically. The camp leader was clutching his sides now, and yelling as if in pain.

Liam slapped himself on the head. 'Dave. Right, of course.' He frowned. 'So, who's—?'

'We don't know!' snapped Sarah.

**109**

Dave clutched his ribs as whatever was under his t-shirt tried to push through it, stretching the fabric. He raised his head until his eyes met Jake's, and Jake took a step back when he saw a faint green glow in their dark centre.

'Oh no,' Jake whispered.

'Oh *yes*,' Dave hissed in reply. 'See, harness the p-power of plants, and you can do anything. You can hide yourself in plain sight. You can bide your time while you plot your revenge on the meddling children who destroyed your army. And then, when the time is right . . .'

There was a loud rip as four branches tore through the back of Dave's t-shirt and sprouted outwards from his body like spider-legs. He straightened with a howl of triumph, then held up his hands as the fingers curved into sharp, stick-like claws.

'Guys!' Liam said. 'I'm not sure, but I think maybe he *is* the Creeper, after all.'

'You don't say,' Sarah whispered, transfixed by the thing that was now half-Dave, half-Creeper. Rough bark was blooming up his neck and spreading across his skin like a rash. His hair was growing, becoming an unkempt tangle of grass and weeds as the green glow of his eyes grew steadily brighter.

'Plan?' Sarah whimpered.

'Fight it?' said Jake, although he didn't sound all that keen.

'Die horribly?' said Liam, who sounded even less enthusiastic.

Sarah shrugged. 'Or we could split the difference and run away?' she suggested.

Jake and Liam exchanged a brief look. They both nodded. 'Yeah,' said Liam. 'Let's do that.'

'I hate to say it,' Jake whispered. 'But what about Callum?'

They all looked down at him. He was still struggling against the vines, but appeared to be in no immediate danger.

'It's us the Creeper wants,' said Sarah.

'Well, *you*, mostly,' Liam said, meeting Jake's eye. 'So I reckon we just leg it, and come back for him later.'

A branch-like arm snapped at them, making them all jump. The Creeper's transformation was complete!

'Sounds good to me!' Jake yelped, and they all turned and ran screaming into the forest, stumbling and tripping as they raced between the trees.

'Oh yes! Flee, children, flee!' the Creeper called after them. He grinned, showing off a mouth full of sharp wooden teeth. A shudder of excitement trembled through his whole body. 'I do so love it

**111**

when they run,' he whispered, then he raised himself up on his spider-leg-like branches, and set off on the hunt for his prey.

## CHAPTER ELEVEN

# DIVIDE AND CONQUER

'Stick together, don't get separated,' Jake cried, throwing his arms up in front of him and barging through a mesh of leafy branches.

Sarah and Liam crashed along behind him, their breaths coming in short, shallow pants as they powered on as fast as their legs would carry them.

'Where are we going?' Sarah wheezed.

'Back to camp,' said Jake. 'Maybe Mr Campion or Lucy can help us!'

'I was worried you might say that,' groaned Sarah, doubling over so she could duck under a low limb.

'Why? What's wrong with going back to camp?' asked Jake, zig-zagging past a mass of prickly bushes.

'Nothing. It's a great plan,' Sarah told him, 'apart

**113**

from one little problem.' She jabbed a thumb back the way they'd come. 'The camp's that way!'

Jake cursed himself below his breath. 'Argh! Why didn't I pay more attention to Mr Campion's navigation lesson on the first day?'

'Because it was really dull?' Liam guessed.

'Yeah,' said Jake, leaping over a knot of knobbly roots. 'That's probably it.'

A deep, rumbling boom from overhead made them all duck with fright.

'Wah!' Liam yelped. 'What was that?'

'Thunder,' said Sarah.

Liam's jaw dropped. 'Wait, he can make thunder now? That's not fair!'

Jake looked up just as a mist of fine rain began to fall. 'I don't think that's the Creeper,' he said. Through the gaps in the branches, he could just make out a layer of grey cloud painted across the night sky. 'I think there's another storm coming.'

Liam shook his head in dismay. 'Never rains but it pours, eh?' he said. 'Literally in this case, I suppose.'

They all stumbled to a stop as the Creeper stepped out from behind a tree in front of them. In his hands, he clutched a dark pink, trumpet-shaped flower. '*Solanaceae brugmansia*,' he announced. 'Able to induce terrifying visions and hallucinations in those who get

**114**

too close.'

With a puff of breath, he launched dozens of colourful pollen spores into the air in front of Jake and the others. They coughed and spluttered as they breathed it in, then Sarah let out a panicky scream.

Jake and Liam whipped around to see a branch grabbing her by the hair and dragging her backwards. Liam's fingers curled into fists. 'Get off my sister!' he roared, then he threw himself at the tree and punched it with all his might.

'Ow! Ow! Ow!' he grimaced, hopping from foot to foot and tucking his hand under the opposite armpit. 'Bad idea!'

Jake spun on the spot, peering into the darkness that seemed to close in around them. The Creeper had vanished, and so had Sarah. 'Where did she go? Sarah? Sarah!'

'Help me!' Sarah shouted, but this time she sounded worryingly far away. Jake and Liam both frantically scanned the shadows, trying to figure out where the cry had come from.

'This way!' they both said, pointing in completely opposite directions.

'You go that way, I'll check over here,' Liam said.

Jake wrung his hands together anxiously. 'This is what he wants. He's trying to split us up.'

But what other choice did they have? Jake nodded to his friend, then set off into the woods. 'Be careful,' he urged. 'And shout if you find her.'

'You too,' said Liam, plunging into the trees. He stumbled on through the darkness, the thin branches scratching and scraping across his face. The cold night air made him shiver, and he was grateful he and his friends had all been sleeping in their clothes. He doubted the Creeper would have given them time to get dressed.

'Sarah?' Liam called. 'Sarah, where are you?'

'Over here,' whispered a voice over on Liam's right. He turned towards it.

'Sarah, is that you?'

'Help me, Liam,' the voice whispered. 'I'm scared.'

'I'm coming, sis!' Liam said. 'Don't worry, I'm coming!'

He charged ahead and immediately smashed face-first into a thick tree trunk. Clutching his nose, he staggered back. 'Ooh, that hurt,' he mumbled, then he took a side-step to the right, lowered his head, and charged off in search of his sister.

Jake, meanwhile, was flailing around in the dark, with no idea where he was. He'd emerged into some kind of clearing, he guessed, but whichever direction he walked in, he couldn't find any trees.

It didn't make sense. The forest was full of trees. It was practically nothing *but* trees. And yet, there were none around him. In fact, there was *nothing* around him, as far as he could tell. It was as if the whole world had vanished, leaving him alone in the dark abyss it left behind.

His heart raced and his breathing became short as he began to panic. He reached ahead, behind, out to both sides, his arms stretching and searching for something—anything—that would tell him where he was. Was he turning in circles? He didn't think so. He was sure he was walking in a straight line, but how else could he explain it? If he was walking in a straight line he'd have hit more trees by now, but all that seemed to be around him was the darkest black he'd ever seen. Or not seen, depending on how you thought about it.

'Sarah? Liam?' he called, but his voice sounded muffled, as if he were in a deep, thick fog that pressed down on him from all sides. The rain was getting heavier. It roared against the canopy of leaves above him, so he knew there had to be trees around somewhere.

But why couldn't he find them?! There was only one explanation.

'I know you're doing this, Creeper!' Jake called.

'Yes,' said a whisper in his ear. 'You're right.'

**117**

Jake turned in the direction of the voice, lashing out with a frantic kick. His foot swished through thin air and he was thrown off balance. He hit the ground backwards and felt the air leave his lungs in one sharp breath.

'Missed me,' whispered the voice again.

Jake tried to stand, but blades of thick grass tangled in his hair, snapping his head back down. The ground squirmed beneath him as weeds and vines wrapped themselves around his wrists, pinning him down.

'Not so fast, Jake,' said the voice in the darkness. 'What's say you and I hang out a little while longer?'

Not too far away, Sarah wrestled against the branches that pinned her arms by her sides. A vine had wrapped around her head, looping under her jaw and holding it shut so she couldn't call for help.

With a grunt of effort, she tried to break free of the branches, but they tightened immediately, slapping her hands against her thighs.

Her right palm bumped against a lump in her pocket. The knife! She still had her Swiss Army knife!

The branches cut into her arm as she struggled to manoeuvre her hand into her pocket. Bending her wrist as far as it would go, she managed to hook the end of one finger into the pocket's narrow opening. She hissed in pain as the branches squeezed, almost snapping her wrist in two.

But she didn't stop. She couldn't stop. Not if she wanted to get out of this in one piece.

Sarah flexed her fingers. If she could just lower her trousers a centimetre or so, she could reach inside the pocket and grab the knife. Then all she had to do was fight off an entire forest with the world's smallest knife, a nail file, and a selection of bottle openers, and everything would be OK.

*Yeah*, she thought. *That's all*.

She was so caught up in trying to reach the knife that she didn't notice the trees ahead of her parting, and a monstrous figure come stepping out of the shadows.

'Well, well, well,' hissed the Creeper. 'Look who we have here.'

'Sarah?' Liam whispered. 'Sarah, where are you?'

'On your left. Quickly!' the voice urged.

'Here I come!' said Liam, picking up the pace.

'Or is it your right?'

Liam about-turned and doubled-back.

'No, left.'

'Make up your mind!' Liam yelped.

The voice began to giggle. It started as a soft hiss, but quickly rose to become a high-pitch shriek of laughter. 'Oh, but it's such fun making you run around like the idiot you are.'

Liam backed away from the direction of the laughter. 'Hang on, you're not Sarah, are you?'

The giggling died away, replaced by an icy-cold hiss. 'Oh, you got me!' said the voice. 'Better run, Liam. I'm coming to get you!'

Liam stumbled away, staggering through the trees, trying to put as much distance between himself and whatever was behind him as possible.

His foot snagged on a root—or maybe the root snagged on him, he couldn't be sure—and he fell forwards into a clearing. He looked up and met the panicky gaze of Callum, still struggling on the ground.

'Alright, Callum?' Liam panted.

Callum's eyebrows knotted in the middle. He began mumbling angrily, and Liam decided it was probably best that he still had the vine gag across his mouth.

'Sorry, can't rescue you right now. Maybe later,' Liam said, jumping up. With a glance behind him to make sure the Creeper wasn't standing there, he hurried to what was left of Sarah's tent and searched

**120**

inside, hoping to find something useful.

His own rucksack was full of comics and the five pairs of pants his mum had packed for him, which he hadn't got round to wearing yet. Neither of those items was likely to help him battle a supernatural plant monster, he decided, so he turned his attention to Sarah's bag.

He quickly found her head torch and flicked the switch to make sure it was working. He hissed as the light shone directly in his eyes, blinding him. Yep, that was definitely working.

Strapping the torch on, he stood up and turned to find Callum standing behind him. 'Hey, you got up!' Liam said, then he yelped as Callum slapped him hard across the face. 'Ow! What did you do that for?'

'It wasn't me,' Callum whimpered.

'It definitely was you!' said Liam. 'I just watched you do it.'

'N-no,' Callum insisted. 'Look!'

He gestured to his wrists. Long, thin vines were wrapped around them, and his ankles, too. The vines stretched up into the dark canopy of leaves overhead. They twitched, making Callum's whole body jerk.

'Ha! You're a puppet!' Liam laughed. His face fell as he gave this some more thought. 'Oh. Hang on. That's not good, is it?'

'Not really, no,' said Callum, then his arm swung up and a powerful right hook sent Liam spinning to the ground.

Jake lay on his back, his arms bent up beside his head, the roots and grass pinning them down. The Creeper's voice whispered from the darkness in all directions, taunting and mocking him.

' . . . let your friends down . . .'

' . . . never get out of here alive . . .'

'Shut up!' Jake hissed through clenched teeth. 'Just shut up!'

This couldn't be real. It couldn't be. The pollen from the Creeper's plant must have done something to them. All this was a dream. It was just in his head, Jake knew, even though the vines pinning him down felt all too real.

'I'm not afraid of you,' he said. 'You're not really the Creeper, and even if you are, you're a coward. You act like you're unstoppable, but you have to use a pathetic sneak attack to try to beat me.'

There was silence from the shadows.

'No, I don't,' said the Creeper, eventually.

'Yes,' said Jake. 'You do. You tried to face us head on back at the school and you couldn't win. You had a whole army behind you and we *still* beat you!'

'Silence!' the Creeper barked, but Jake was on a roll now.

'Think about it. The first time we met you tried to kill me,' Jake said, smirking. 'And how did I beat you? Remind me again.'

'Shut up!' hissed the darkness from three different directions at once.

'Not with a gun. Not with a sword,' said Jake.

'Ssshut up!'

'But with a packet of salt and vinegar crisps,' said Jake. 'In fact, no. *Half* a packet of salt and vinegar crisps. So, I suppose it's fair enough that you're too scared to face me properly,' he said, shrugging. 'If I were you, I'd be terrified, too.'

The vines pinning Jake to the ground slithered away, leaving him free to jump to his feet. The rain poured down and a rumble of thunder rolled across the sky, followed a moment later by a flash of electric blue.

For a split second, the clearing was illuminated. Jake could see the trees now, and realized to his horror that several of the trunks had twisted to form faces. Or, more accurately, one specific face.

'You want to face me, Jake?' said the Creeper from

several directions at once. 'Pick a face!'

'Actually,' said Jake. 'All that stuff I said about fighting you? I was bluffing. You're well scary. See you!'

He turned in what he hoped was a Creeper-free direction and, powered entirely by panic, flung himself into the nightmare forest, shouting at himself to wake up.

## CHAPTER TWELVE

# AN UNFRIENDLY WAVE

Sarah looked up at the sound of the Creeper's voice. The figure skulked towards her, the spider-like branch-legs on his back carrying him across the narrow clearing.

'What do you want?' Sarah demanded. 'Let me go.'

'Hmm . . . no, I don't think so,' said the Creeper. 'I think I'll keep you right where you are.'

He stepped closer, and the smell of tree sap snagged at the back of Sarah's throat. 'You three are a real nuisance, you know that?' said the Creeper, accusingly. 'And you're the brains of the bunch. Not that that's exactly saying much.'

'We stopped you before, Creeper, and we'll stop you again!'

The monster's leafy eyebrows knotted angrily. 'I don't know if you're very brave, or very stupid,' he said.

Sarah shrugged. It was much easier, now that she'd sneakily managed to cut through the thin branches that had been holding her to the tree. 'Maybe I'm both. But I'm something else, too,' she said.

'Oh? And what's that?' asked the Creeper.

'Armed!' said Sarah. Lunging forwards, she swished her tiny pen knife at the villain. A thick, branch-like arm raised, blocking the attack. The figure opened its mouth wide, and Sarah screamed as dozens of woodlice came scuttling out and dropped to the forest floor between them.

Pulling away, Sarah dodged a swiping vine attack, then raced off into the dark forest, not daring to look back.

Liam danced around, his fists held in front of his face like he was pretty sure he'd seen a boxer do on telly once, after he'd accidentally turned to the wrong sports channel while searching for the FA Cup Final.

'Cut it out, Callum, I'm warning you!' he said. 'These hands are deadly weapons. They will mess you up!'

**127**

'I keep telling you, it's not me!' said Callum. His left hand swished up and cracked Liam with a slap across the jaw. 'It's the trees! The trees are alive!'

'Ooh yes, that's what you'd like me to think, isn't it?' said Liam, straightening his head torch and trying his best to ignore the burning on his face where Callum's hand had connected. 'I mean . . . obviously I can see that it's true, but don't try to tell me you're not loving every minute of it.'

'OK, fine. Yes, I am. I'm loving every minute of it,' Callum confessed. 'Happy?'

Roaring, Liam swung with an overhead punch. Callum jerked upwards on the vines then glided gracefully through the air as Liam stumbled off-balance and smashed his fist into the trunk of a tree.

'You totally telegraphed that,' Callum said, landing lightly on the forest floor behind Liam. 'Stop making it so obvious. Anyone could have seen that punch coming!'

'Liam! Liam, wake up!' Jake's voice drifted towards Liam on the breeze.

'Huh?' said Liam. 'What are you talking about? I am awake!'

'Snap out of it! It's not real. Whatever you're seeing, it's not real!'

Liam looked Callum up and down. 'Hey, puppet-

Callum, are you real?'

Callum shrugged. 'No,' he admitted. 'Sorry.'

'Oh,' said Liam. 'Oh, right. Well, that's a relief.'

Liam sat up with a gasp, his eyes bulging. He was lying on his back in the woods, Jake shaking him violently by the shoulders.

'Ow! Cut it out!' Liam yelped. He rubbed his face. 'Did you slap me?'

'Just once,' said Jake. 'Maybe twice.'

A flash of lightning illuminated the sky right above them. The thunder followed just a second later—a roaring *boom* that shook leaves from trees. The rattling of the raindrops on the treetops was deafening, and as the rain poured down, Sarah sat up with a shriek of fright.

'Sarah! You're alive!' Liam threw his arms around his sister and hugged her so hard her eyes almost popped. He held her like that until she thought she was about to pass out from lack of oxygen, then released his grip and stepped back.

'I mean, hey,' he said, nonchalantly.

Sarah smiled. 'Hey yourself.'

They jumped to their feet and searched the clearing. 'I just had the craziest dream,' said Sarah.

'Yeah, I think it was that plant the Creeper used on us. It made us hallucinate,' Jake explained. 'It either

**129**

wore off or the rain washed it away.'

'Unless this is still a dream, too!' said Liam. He nipped himself hard on the arm. 'Ow! No, I think this is real. That really hurt.'

'So where is he now?' asked Sarah.

'I don't know,' said Jake.

'And why didn't he finish us off when he had the chance?'

'Maybe he wants to toy with us, and make us scared,' Jake guessed.

Liam whimpered. 'Then he's doing a very good job of it.'

'You can say that again,' Jake whispered. 'Let's get out of here before he comes back!'

'Brilliant plan, let's do it!' said Liam, and they all broke into a run.

The canopy of trees stopped much of the rain coming through, but the forest floor was still slick and slippy as they scrambled across it. They ran side-by-side where possible, falling into single file wherever the trees grew closer together.

'I wish I still had that head torch,' said Liam, as they stumbled through the shadows.

'What head torch?' asked Sarah.

'The one I was wearing a minute ago,' Liam explained. 'When I was fighting Callum.'

'In the dream you mean?' said Jake. '*That* head torch?'

'Yes!' said Liam. 'Any idea where it went?'

Jake sighed. There was no point trying to explain. 'It probably fell off,' he said.

'I think I can see the edge of the woods,' Sarah announced, squinting as she peered through the gaps in the trees ahead.

'Brilliant! Are we at the camp?' Jake asked, panting from the effort of running so fast and so far.

'Can't be,' said Sarah. 'It's somewhere back that way.'

The trees and foliage thinned. 'Then where are we?' Jake asked.

Just ahead of him, Liam skidded to a stop. A vast expanse of dark water lay dead ahead of them, the rain dotting its surface with thousands of slowly expanding circles.

'I think it's the lake,' said Liam.

'Observant as ever,' said Sarah.

'It's a dead end, we have to go back,' Jake realized. They all spun on the spot, but before they could take a step, the trees ahead of them bent apart, the ancient trunks groaning with the strain as they parted to form a path.

'If you go down to the woods today, you're sure of a big surprise . . .' sang the Creeper, as he stalked through

**131**

the gap on his branch-legs.

'Can't go that way!' Sarah yelped. 'Only one thing for it!'

'Swim for it!' cried Liam, hurling himself into the lake. He landed with a faint splash in ankle-deep water. 'OK, that was supposed to be much more dramatic,' he confessed, then he yelped as Sarah caught him by the arm and yanked him back onto dry land.

'No, not swim. *Paddle*,' she said, jabbing a finger to the little jetty further along the shore. The kayaks were tied up there, bobbing and clunking together as the wind pushed them around.

'Yeah. Yeah, that's definitely better,' Liam admitted, as they all raced for the row of boats.

'Here,' said Jake, throwing open a metal box and tossing his friends a life jacket each. 'Better safe than sorry.'

'Hey, look! My life jacket has a little torch hooked to it. Bonus!' said Liam. He switched it on, dazzled himself, and immediately switched it off again. 'I do love a little torch.'

Fastening their jackets, they all grabbed one of the long metal paddles and slipped into their kayaks. Sarah hung back a little to unhook the ropes, before sliding into her own boat and pushing away from the jetty.

'Hurry, this way!' she said, paddling frantically. A

flicker of lightning illuminated the Creeper. He was almost at the shore now, his face twisting into a furious scowl. 'He can't get us out on the water. We'll be safe.'

Thunder exploded above them like a bomb blast, rippling the water on all sides. Liam glanced upwards. 'Funnily enough, I don't feel particularly safe,' he said, wobbling around on his kayak. 'This was tricky enough when we weren't caught in a storm in the middle of the night!'

Out there, away from the trees, the rain lashed at them, slicking their skin and plastering their hair to their heads. They powered on with their paddles, Sarah holding back so the boys could keep up.

'Just a little farther,' she said. 'He won't be able to reach us.'

Another flash of lightning lit up the sky. This time, it tore down from the clouds in a jagged fork. A tree exploded in a shower of sparks and burning leaves. The flaming debris fluttered to the ground, briefly illuminating the Creeper once more.

He was crouching down right at the edge of the shore now, his hands plunged into the icy water.

'What's he up to?' Jake wondered.

'Maybe he's just washing his hands,' Liam guessed.

'I doubt he'd take a break from trying to kill us just to wash his hands,' said Sarah.

**133**

'Some people take personal hygiene very seriously,' said Liam. 'I mean, not me, obviously, but some people do.'

A wave rippled towards them, rushing at their boats from the shore. The kayaks bobbed madly in the water for a moment, before the wave rolled past them.

'What was that?' asked Jake.

'Just a wave, I think,' said Liam. 'Nothing to worry about.'

'Except waves generally go *towards* the shore,' Sarah pointed out.

Liam swallowed. 'Oh. Right. Well, in that case, maybe it is something to worry about.'

Another wave crashed across the kayaks, rocking them violently. Jake yelped as his boat began to tip, but Sarah managed to bump him upright just in the nick of time.

KER-ACK!

Another fork of lightning ripped across the sky, striking the metal box where the life jackets were stored. For a moment, Jake thought he saw something below the water, but then the flash was gone and darkness returned.

'Liam,' Jake whispered. 'Shine that torch on the water.'

Something about the tone of Jake's voice made

Liam hesitate. 'Um . . . no, thanks,' he said.

'What?' Jake frowned.

'You sound scared, so I bet if I shine this down there I'm going to see something terrifying, like a big octopus or a shark or an underwater lion, or something,' Liam explained. 'So, if it's all the same with you, I'm not going to bother.'

Sarah leaned over and snatched the torch from Liam's life jacket. 'Give it here!' she said, clicking it on and angling the beam towards the water's surface. A forest of green swept back and forth below them, building up speed as it flicked towards the shore and back again.

'It's the pond weed,' Sarah gasped. 'He's taken control of the pond weed and he's using it to make the—'

Another wave smashed into them. It was much larger and stronger than the others, and even Sarah could do nothing but close her eyes and hold her breath as all three kayaks were flipped over.

The water was cold. Very cold. Much colder than Jake had been expecting. Instinctively, he began to gasp, but he realized that opening his mouth underwater probably wasn't the best idea, and managed to force it to stay closed. His feet moved on their own, kicking out frantically as he struggled to free himself from the kayak.

**137**

The darkness of the lake was all around him, squeezing him, squashing him. He could feel the pond weed flick across his face, could hear the commotion as Liam and Sarah wrestled with their own boats.

And then, all of a sudden, he broke the surface. His mouth opened and the air he'd swallowed down escaped in one big gasp. Sarah's head popped up next to him. She panted heavily, shivering in the cold.

'Liam?' Jake called, thrashing around in the water. 'Liam, where are you?'

'Over here!' called Liam from somewhere closer to the shore. They could just make him out, moving quickly through the water, his arms flailing above his head.

Pond weed wrapped around Jake's ankle. Sarah cried out as she felt the thick oily greenery tangle her feet, too. With a yank, they were both pulled towards the shore. Jake tried to front crawl towards his kayak, but the weeds yanked him away.

'Grab a paddle!' Jake said. 'Hurry!'

Sarah snatched for one of the long paddles as the weeds pulled her through the water. Her fingertips brushed against the hollow metal, and for a horrible moment she thought she'd missed. But then she caught the flat plastic end, and managed to hold on.

'Got it!' she said. 'But I don't think it's much good

without the kayak.'

'We'll see,' Jake said. He reached across and took the paddle from her, just as the water became land and they rolled to a stop on the shore.

'Liam, y-you OK?' asked Jake.

Liam, who was lying flat on his back, raised one hand, gave a thumbs up, then let it collapse again. Sarah began to get to her feet, but Jake shook his head. 'Stay down,' he whispered. 'Whatever happens, stay down.'

And then, using the oar for support, Jake shakily stood up, and found himself face to face with the Creeper.

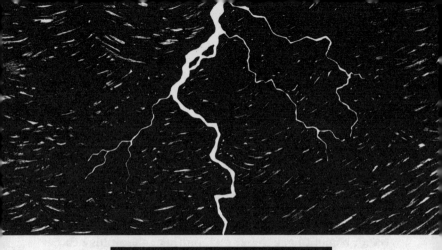

## CHAPTER THIRTEEN

# STRIKE OUT

The thin beam of the torch shone on the Creeper from below, casting his bark-covered face into sinister shadow. The monster's glowing green eyes fixed hungrily on Jake, as a sickening smirk slithered across his face.

'Ah, here we all are, together again,' said the Creeper. 'Isn't this nice?'

'Not particularly,' voiced Liam from down on the ground.

'Speak for yourself,' said the Creeper. 'I'm very much enjoying our little reunion.'

He leaned in closer so his face was closer to Jake's. Jake could smell the mulchy musk of decay whenever the Creeper opened his mouth which, unfortunately, was quite often. 'And I'm going to enjoy it even more in a moment,' the monster whispered.

'What's your plan this time, Creeper?' Jake demanded.

'Plan? Yes, I suppose I probably should have a plan, shouldn't I?' the villain said. 'To be honest, though, I haven't really thought beyond killing you three. That's pretty much been entirely my focus since our last encounter.'

'Is it weird that I'm quite flattered by that?' asked Liam.

'Yes,' said Sarah.

Jake tightened his grip on the paddle and cast a nervous glance towards the sky. 'Although, I should thank you all, I suppose,' the Creeper said. 'I thought my army of potato-people was the perfect means with which to take over the world, but I can see now how naïve it was. Childish, almost.'

He snorted a laugh from his wooden nose. 'I mean . . . really. Soldiers made from potatoes? It's almost comical.'

'Oh yeah, it was a right barrel of laughs,' Liam chipped in.

'SILENCE!' the Creeper roared, and the forest itself seemed to tremble at his voice.

'OK then, fine,' said Liam weakly. 'But only because

**141**

I was going to shut up, anyway.'

The Creeper turned his attention back to Jake, who was stealing another glance up at the storm clouds above them. 'I didn't need to build an army,' the Creeper continued. 'I *have* an army already at my disposal, and once I've taken care of you three, I can put them to work.'

He turned on the spot, gesturing to the world in general. 'Every tree, every plant, every tiny flower budding into bloom—they're all mine to do with as I choose. I can shape them, bend them to my will. I'm really rather impressive, you know?'

'You said you wanted to protect plants, not use them as slaves,' Sarah reminded him.

The Creeper shrugged. 'Things change. Once they've served me and helped me eliminate or dominate all mankind—haven't quite decided which, yet—then they'll be free. Truly free. Free of the torture and abuse inflicted by the human race. Free of the pruning. Chopping. Harvesting. It will all finally end.'

'And until then you'll just keep using them however you like?' said Sarah.

The Creeper tutted. 'You can't make an omelette without breaking some eggs,' he said. 'Will I manipulate the flora and force it to do my evil bidding? Yes, *obviously*. Will it be for its own good in the long

**142**

run? Yes. Of course.'

'I don't think you do care about the plants, Creeper,' Jake said, his eyes darting briefly skyward again. The fine hairs on the back of his neck stood on end as the air pressure around the group changed. 'I think you just want power.'

The Creeper's smirk widened, showing off his dirty brown teeth. 'You know, Jake,' he sniggered. 'You might be right. Maybe, deep down, that's all I do want. Unfortunately for you, you won't be around to find out.'

'Oh, I think we will!' Jake cried. He swung at the monster with the paddle, aiming the hard plastic blade at his head. It was heavier than it looked, though, and the rushing wind made swinging it harder than Jake had expected.

'Nice try,' said the Creeper, easily blocking the attack. He grabbed the metal pole and plucked it from Jake's hands. 'Not exactly a deadly weapon, is it?'

Jake glanced anxiously at the sky. 'It wasn't meant to be a weapon,' he said. 'Look closely.'

Frowning, the Creeper raised the paddle and looked along its length. 'What am I supposed to be looking at here? I don't see anything. If you weren't using it as a weapon, what was it supposed to be?'

'A lightning rod,' said Jake, then he threw himself

to the ground just as a bright blue fork of electricity tore the sky in two.

'Ooh, this is going to hurt,' the Creeper managed to groan, just before the lightning hit the metal paddle in a shower of crackling sparks.

'You want power, Creeper? Let's see how much you can handle!' Jake cried, then he, Sarah, and Liam covered their heads with their hands as the monster was illuminated in a blinding blue glow.

There was a FZZT.

There was a BANG!

And then there was nothing but the sound of falling rain, and the unmistakable smell of burning wood.

Jake and the others raised their heads. The paddle lay on the ground, the plastic ends melted, the metal pole bent into an uneven curve. Where the Creeper had stood there was now just a blackened scorch mark on the grass.

'Is . . . is he gone?' Liam whispered.

Sarah glanced around. 'I think so,' she said. 'Can't see him anywhere.'

Liam bounded to his feet. 'Eat *that*, Creeper!' he cried. A loud *boom* crashed above them, and Liam threw himself to the ground again. 'I'm sorry, I'm sorry, don't kill me!' he whimpered.

'Relax, it's just thunder,' said Jake, getting to his

feet. 'We did it. We stopped him again.'

Sarah stood up and gave the area one more check. 'He's gone.'

'For now, anyway,' said Jake, peering into the shadowy forest. 'But why do I have a nasty feeling that we haven't seen the last of him?'

When Jake and the others arrived back at camp, they were met by a scene of utter chaos. Kids were running around, trying to catch their flying tents. The toilet block had blown over, spilling smelly chemicals—and worse—all over the logs where they sat to eat their meals.

Lucy was wading through ankle-deep mud, trying to help gather everyone's things together, while Mr Campion stood in the middle, barking orders and ushering everyone onto the minibus.

'What happened?' Jake asked. Mr Campion shot him a withering look.

'Rain came on. Got a bit blowy. Perhaps you noticed?'

Jake looked up, as if only seeing the rain for the first time. 'Yeah. OK. I mean . . . was that all?'

'*All*?' yelped Lucy, as she squelched past, trying to catch a flying rucksack. 'It's the storm of the century.'

'Yes, but I mean, a monster didn't do all this?' Jake asked, gesturing around at the carnage.

'Not more monster-talk! When are you going to get it into your heads that there's no such thing?' demanded Mr Campion. He pointed to a girl who was struggling to fold her tent down. 'Abandon it. It's too late to save it. Get on the bus at once!'

'He was here,' Liam blurted.

'The Creeper,' said Jake. 'The one who attacked the school.'

Mr Campion's nostrils flared. 'Oh, not this nonsense again,' he said.

'It's true!' said Jake.

'He made himself look like Terry!' said Liam.

'Dave!' Sarah cried, throwing her hands in the air. 'And *no*, we still don't know who Terry is.'

Mr Campion scowled. 'Look, we don't have time for this tomfoolery ...'

'Wait! Wait!' Jake yelped, bouncing up and down. 'Callum! Callum saw him. He can back us up.'

The head glanced around the camp. 'Fine. Where is he?'

Jake's face fell. 'Um ... he's out there somewhere,' he said, pointing in the direction of the rotten old tent.

**146**

'But he might be a puppet,' added Liam, helpfully.

Mr Campion's jaw dropped. He glared at the children for several long seconds, before shaking his head. 'Get on the bus,' he told them. 'I'll go and find Callum.'

They watched him go, then Liam and Jake turned towards the minibus. They had to lean forwards into the wind just to take a few small steps. Sarah hung back. 'Wait. What about my tent?'

'Just leave it,' said Jake, shouting to make himself heard over the howling gale.

'But it's expensive!' Sarah protested. 'It took me almost a year to save up for it.'

'Do you really want to go back out into the woods to get it?' Jake asked.

Sarah considered this. 'On second thoughts,' she said, 'last one to the bus is a rotten egg.'

'Leg,' Liam corrected.

'It's *egg*,' Sarah said, as they all lowered their heads and ran into the wind. 'It's *rotten egg*.'

Liam laughed. 'As if. It's rotten *leg*. Isn't it, Jake? It definitely is. Jake?'

Jake just smiled and hurried on. They'd done it. They'd stopped the Creeper once again. He and his friends had saved the day, and once Callum told everyone what had happened, people would *have* to believe them.

'What do you mean "he doesn't remember"?'

Mr Campion shrugged. 'I don't know any other way to put it,' the head said. 'Remember he does not. Is that any clearer?'

Jake leaned back in his seat and groaned. Mr Campion had come running into camp just a few minutes before, carrying an embarrassed-looking Callum in his arms. He looked like a hero rescuing a damsel in distress in an old movie, and Liam had even hummed a dramatic Hollywood soundtrack as they'd watched the head teacher race towards the minibus.

Callum had a big lump on his head from where he'd been hit by a flying branch. He claimed to have no memory of going into the forest, and knew nothing about any monster.

'Does he remember what happened to my head torch?' Liam asked.

'That was a dream!' Sarah sighed.

'He's lying. He's got to be,' said Jake, as the head crisply about-turned, then marched to the front of the bus and slid into the driver's seat.

'Who, Mr Campion?' said Liam. 'I don't think

**148**

teachers are allowed to lie, are they? It's the law.'

'No, not Mr Campion, Callum,' said Jake. 'I bet he does remember, but just isn't telling.'

'I don't know,' said Sarah. 'That lump on his head does look pretty enormous. Amnesia is a possibility.'

Lucy squelched along the bus in her muddy boots, counting everyone. 'Thirteen, fourteen. That's everyone!' she called, and the bus rumbled as the engine roared into life.

'Not everyone,' said Jake.

'We haven't got Dave,' said Sarah.

'Because he turned into a massive monster,' added Jake.

Lucy scraped her hair back and squeezed some of the water out of it. 'What are you on about? Dave quit yesterday and went home. Said he couldn't be dealing with annoying kids any more.' She shook her head. 'Couldn't believe it. I mean, you're not annoying!'

She shot Liam the briefest of brief glances. 'I mean, very few of you are annoying,' she corrected.

'But . . . no. But . . .' Jake said. 'He . . . we saw him. He turned into a tree man.'

All of a sudden, Lucy produced her ukulele from somewhere. She twanged the strings. It made a sound like a startled cat.

'Tree man, oh tree man, oh where could you be,

**149**

man?' she sang. 'I'm out here in the forest, having lots of fun!'

Jake, Sarah, Liam, and everyone else on the bus wriggled down in their seats, trying to block out the sound of Lucy's singing. The bus rocked and rolled as Mr Campion steered it onto the track that led towards the main road.

Jake gazed out through the window, watching the dark woods flash by. Across the aisle, Lucy continued to strum and warble.

' . . . and skip and jump and hop. For I am the tree man . . . and I will never stop!'

The woods became a blur as Mr Campion pressed down on the accelerator, and the bus pushed onwards into the oncoming storm.

## CHAPTER FOURTEEN

# Hacker's Final Thoughts

When I heard about the storm ruining the school camping expedition, I didn't really pay too much attention. It wasn't until I overheard someone mention Jake, Sarah, and Liam that I knew I had to look into the story a little more closely.

I snooped around a little at first, and tried to speak to the camp leaders. Lucy didn't prove particularly helpful, especially when she started singing the answers to all my questions. At least, I think she was singing. Either that or she was in considerable pain. The other camp leader, Dave, was nowhere to be found.

In fact, the more I looked into him, the less I

discovered. The address the camp company had on file for him turned out to be a gardening supply shop, and the phone number wasn't recognized. I've dug around a lot, tapped all my sources, but from what I can gather, Dave either disappeared completely, or didn't really exist in the first place. I'm not really sure which is weirder.

Callum told me he didn't remember anything after lunchtime on the day of the storm. His friend, Matthew, claims he headed off to set up some sort of prank when everyone else was sitting eating around the campfire, but Callum doesn't remember that at all. So he says, at least, and I'm inclined to believe him. The lump he got on his head from that fallen tree branch is pretty enormous, after all.

So, to cut a long story short, I was met with a whole lot of dead ends. Until, that is, I spoke to Jake, Liam, and Sarah, and got the real story from them.

As soon as they mentioned the pond weed turning into a wave machine, I knew the Creeper had to be behind it. Sure enough, they told me everything— from their terrifying hallucinations in the woods, to their final confrontation on the lake shore.

I have to say, using the metal paddle as a lightning rod was an inspired move, and I hoped it meant we'd seen the last of the Creeper.

*As the monster told Jake, Liam, and Sarah, though—no matter how far you cut a plant down, they can always grow back. The Creeper wasn't dead. Hurt, yes, but dead? Not by a long shot.*

*He was recovering. Healing up. Mending himself.*

*Changing himself, too, thanks to his terrifying new ability to become anyone he chose.*

*Jake suspected the Creeper would return, and he was right. And, when he did come back, they would discover just how monstrous he truly was . . .*

*But that's a tale for another time. For now, keep your eyes on your shrubberies, and be wary of your veg. The Creeper is still out there, looking for his next victim.*

*Looking, perhaps, for you.*

*Your friend,*
Hacker Murphy

**153**

ARE YOU BRAVE ENOUGH
TO HANDLE MORE
CREEPER FILES?

READ ON FOR A TASTE OF

THE ROOT OF ALL EVIL.

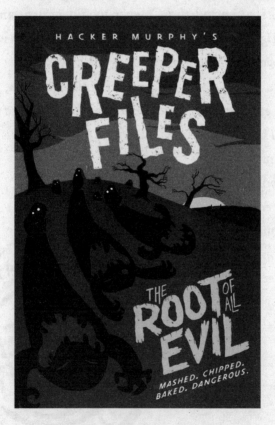

AVAILABLE NOW.

The giant head of broccoli rose up from the water, steam rising from every twisted stem and glistening crown. For a second, it paused, allowing any excess liquid to run away along its thick, green torso. Then it turned to face its prey: a boy, playing on his mobile phone, unaware of the threat posed by this vast victim-seeking vegetable.

Finally free of the water, the broccoli was lifted up into the air. It seemed to shiver—maybe from the change in temperature, but perhaps from the anticipation of the moment when it would appear before its unsuspecting quarry.

THUMP!

The bulging bulk of brassica landed squarely in front of the boy. He recoiled, dropping his phone and opening his mouth to cry out . . .

'There's no way I'm eating that much broccoli, Mum!' exclaimed Jake Latchford, bending to pick up his phone. He gave his dog, Max, a quick tickle behind the ears while his hand was under the table.

'Then you won't be getting any dessert afterwards, will you?' replied Mum.

'But, look at it!' cried Jake. 'It's so big it's bending light around itself. I can't even see my chicken and potatoes any more. This thing should have its own moon!'

'You can moan all you want,' Mum said, placing the gravy boat in the centre of the table and taking her seat. 'But you're not leaving this room until you've eaten all your vegetables.'

'Vegetables?' beamed Dad, hurrying in and dropping into his own chair. 'Yum! The more the merrier for me, please!'

Jake's eyes lit up. 'You can have this big bit of—'

'Jake!' snapped Mum. 'Don't you dare. Eat your broccoli, then you can have some ice cream.'

'What flavour ice cream is it?'

'Cabbage,' said Dad with a grin. 'With sprout sprinkles.'

'You'd eat that, wouldn't you?' said Jake, shuddering.

Dad nodded. 'Too right!'

Despite his mood, Jake smiled. 'Weirdo!'

'Vegetable dodger!'

'No one's dodging anything,' warned Mum. 'And

don't think you can get rid of your dinner by feeding it to Max under the table, either.'

Jake lifted his hand from his lap and dropped the stem of broccoli back onto his plate. 'How did you know?' he asked.

'She's a mother,' said Dad through a mouthful of roast potato. 'Trust me. They know. They know everything.'

Jake picked up his knife and fork. He held them, poised above the steaming pile of greenery. 'Oh well,' he said, suddenly not very hungry. 'Here goes.'

Twenty long, agonizing minutes later, Jake forced the final piece of broccoli into his mouth and chewed hard. Several hours seemed to pass until the lump was small enough to swallow.

'There!' he groaned, sliding his cutlery onto the empty plate. 'I finished it. But if I have some sort of allergic reaction and turn green in the middle of the night, it's all your fault.'

'Well, if that happens, we'll charge people a pound to come and see the amazing vegetable boy,' said Dad. 'Now, about that ice cream . . .'

'It's chocolate,' said Mum. 'But first—one of you can help me clear the plates away, and the other can take Max around the block.'

Both Jake and his dad grabbed their plates and

stood. Mum shook her head and carried her own plate to the sink.

'We can't both clear the table,' said Jake.

'Let's toss for it,' said Dad. 'Heads or tails?'

'Tails!'

'I don't actually have a coin,' Dad confessed. 'Mum, heads or tails?'

'Heads,' said Mum.

Dad gave Jake a sympathetic pat on the shoulder. 'Oh, hard lines,' he said, trying not to laugh. 'Looks like you're walking off all that broccoli!'

With a groan, Jake grabbed Max's lead from the hook by the back door. 'It's just not my night, is it? Come on, boy . . .'

But Max wouldn't move. Instead he sat, glaring at the back door, and snarling.

'Max!' groaned Jake. 'I'm not in the mood for this. Come on!'

More snarls.

Sighing, Jake pulled on his coat and clipped Max's lead to his collar. He gave the lead a tug—but still Max stayed exactly where he was. 'What's wrong with him? He's usually desperate to get outside.'

Dad shrugged as he reached for the now-empty gravy boat. 'Could be that new cat they've got at number 19. She's been winding him up all week—

walking up and down on the fence like she owns the place.'

'He tries to get to her, but his legs are too little,' said Mum, whispering the words in case she hurt Max's feelings. 'Bless.'

'Well, cat or no cat—we're going out!' Jake reached out with his free hand to open the back door, then he pulled Max across the lino towards the exit with all his might.

'Don't forget to check my new petunias while you're out there,' said Mum. 'They were doing quite well the last time I looked.'

'Petunias,' said Jake. 'What colour are those ones again?'

'Pink,' said Mum. 'Well, pinkish-purple. Well, sort of purpley with a kind of lilac undertone to them.'

Jake blinked. 'Pink. Right. I'll take a look,' he said, practically dragging his dog out into the fresh air.

Outside, Max became even more upset. He began to bark madly and pull Jake along the garden towards the gate.

'I don't get it!' cried Jake. 'First you don't want to go out at all, and now you can't wait for your walk. I wish you'd make your mind up!'

Max continued to bark, his ears lying flat against his head, and eyes darting back and forth.

'Suit yourself!' said Jake, looping the lead over the gatepost. 'Wait here for a minute while I check on Mum's flowers.'

Hurrying back up the garden, Jake kneeled on the cold grass and used the light from his mobile phone to check on his mum's budding flowers—but they weren't there. Instead, he found a handful of torn green leaves and the occasional pink or purple petal.

'Oh no,' said Jake to himself. 'Not again!'

Three times now in the past six weeks, someone had attacked gardens in this neighbourhood at night, tearing up flower beds, and generally ruining all the hard work put into their greenery by his mum and all their neighbours.

At first, blame was laid directly at the feet of young ruffians. The young ruffians quickly got together to issue a statement in which they denied any involvement in the garden-wrecking, and threatened to kick the heads in of anyone who said different. After that, everyone stopped pointing the finger their way.

Jake stood up and peered out into the darkness of the street, searching for—well, something that looked suspicious. The trouble was that everything looked suspicious in the fizzing yellow glow of the ancient street lamps. Even Dad's tool shed on the far side of the lawn had a distinct air of malice about it at night, and the worst thing that had ever happened in there was the time Dad's barrel of home brew ginger beer had exploded while he was testing the mixture. It took over a week of showers before the local cats would stop following him everywhere he went.

Glancing back at the house, Jake briefly considered heading back inside to tell his mum what had happened, but knew she wouldn't be happy if he didn't take Max out on his walk first. He fished a slightly crushed bag of salt and vinegar crisps out of his pocket and tore it open, eager to rid his taste buds of the lingering aftermath of broccoli. He tipped the bag up to his mouth, when—

CRASH!

The sound had come from further down the street. Could the flower-flattening fiend still be here? Still up to his wicked work? There was only one way to find out . . .

Easing the gate open, Jake slipped the crisp packet back into his pocket and allowed Max to lead him out into the street. The dog pulled and pulled, something he would normally be told off for, but on this occasion Jake welcomed both Max's keen nose, and the fact that he could look quite big and scary under the right lights—and these were indeed the right lights.

So he let Max tug him along the road in the

direction of the sound. Jake peered over walls and fences as they hurried along. Each one had been attacked by whoever—or whatever—was doing this. Plants had been torn up at the roots and scattered over lawns. Snapped stems and pulverized petals were all that remained of carefully tended flower beds. And, in one garden, the little gnome sitting at the edge of the pond had had his fishing rod snapped in half.

Was there no end to the evil currently stalking Larkspur?

Max picked up the pace. Jake could feel his heart pumping in his chest, and his palms were growing sweaty. Quite what he would do if he did stumble across a gang of motorbike-owning, tulip-despising ne'er-do-wells he didn't rightly know. Maybe it was time to arrange some backup.

Grabbing his mobile phone from his pocket, he hit speed-dial 2, clamped the phone to his ear, and tried to hear the ringing sound over the noise of Max's excited panting.

Eventually, the line connected with a CLICK!

'Liam,' Jake hissed. 'It's me.'

'Jake-a-roo!' cried Liam's tinny voice through the phone's speaker. 'I was expecting you to call . . .'

'You were?'

'Obviously! I mean—come on . . . You must have

installed the new power pack for *Brick-Quest* by now! What do you think of it?'

Jake sighed. Of course. This evening was when the latest upgrade to their favourite computer game was due to be released. With the battle of the broccoli— and now a potential monster on the loose—he'd forgotten all about it.

'Well . . .'

'Tell me you've at least downloaded it!'

'Sorry, no . . .' said Jake. 'I'm out at the moment, walking Max.'

'Running Max by the sounds of it mate, you're out of breath.'

'Yeah,' gasped Jake. 'He's really going for it tonight.'

'So, if it's not to tell me that *Brick-Quest 2.8* is the best version of the game ever, why did you ring me?'

'It's the gardens again,' said Jake, 'they're—'

He stopped as Max's ears flattened back and he began to growl softly.

'What is it, boy?' hissed Jake, peering into the darkness.

And then he saw it. Standing in the next-to-last garden of the street was a tall, extremely thin figure, silhouetted in the harsh yellow streetlight on the corner. The man—and it had to be a man—bent over and Jake could hear the unmistakable sound of flower stems breaking as the figure tore them from the ground.

Then slowly, deliberately, the man raised the handful of tattered blooms to his mouth—and he began to eat them. The figure chewed carefully as though he was savouring the flavours of a gourmet meal.

Then, Max barked. The man's head jerked in their direction, tendrils of half-eaten greenery dangling

from between his teeth. Then he turned and started to walk towards them.

Pulling hard on Max's lead, Jake swung open the nearest garden gate and led his pet down onto a well-maintained lawn beyond. Like the other gardens, ruined flower beds said the thin man had been here as well, presumably making a meal of the owner's hard work. But he hadn't touched a thick hedge standing sentry near the front door of the house. Warning Max to stay silent, Jake pulled him behind the hedge.

The tall, thin man came closer—easing his way along the street while finishing off his fistful of flowers. Jake still couldn't make them out, but he could tell that the man's eyes were sweeping the shadows, searching for him. The creature was sniffing at the air too, as though he could discern the scent of living flesh from partially-devoured foliage.

All Jake had to do was stay absolutely silent, and he would be—

**BEEP BEEP! BEEP BEEP!**

Jake stared in horror as a text message lit up the screen of his phone. It was from Liam . . .

'You can design your own bricks!'

The figure spun to look straight at Jake. And this time he could see the figure's eyes.

They were glowing bright green.

# Ready for more great stories?
# Try one of these...

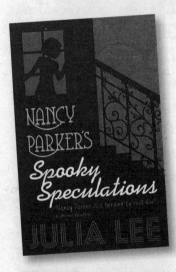